**To my son, Matt,
who was both my best listener
and my toughest critic**

Meet Calliope Day

Charles Haddad

Illustrated by Steve Pica

A Yearling Book

Published by
Bantam Doubleday Dell Books for Young Readers
a division of
Random House, Inc.
1540 Broadway
New York, New York 10036

Visit us on the Web! www.randomhouse.com

**Educators and librarians, for a variety of teaching tools, visit us at
www.randomhouse.com/teachers**

ISBN 0-440-41409-1

Reprinted by arrangement with Delacorte Press

Printed in the United States of America

September 1999

10 9 8 7 6 5 4 3 2 1

CWO

Defanged

Now, mind you, Calliope Day had never bitten anyone in the neck. Oh, she had thought about it. She'd thought about it a lot. Guess what? She was thinking about it right now, right here in class.

"Where are they?" Calliope whispered to herself.

She sat upright, eyes ahead at the chalkboard. Her hand groped inside the red backpack resting against her knee.

She felt pencils, a pencil sharpener, rubber bands, books—*ooh, chewed gum*—and hairbands. She felt something hard, plastic and sharp. Smiling, she wrapped her fingers around it. Her hand rose slowly out of the backpack. There was a flash of pink as she slipped something into her mouth.

Calliope looked around quickly. Everyone had

their eyes on Mrs. Perkins, who was writing on the chalkboard.

Calliope hissed and snapped once at the air, revealing a mouthful of plastic fangs. She looked around quickly again. All eyes were still on the chalkboard.

Calliope scanned the rows of necks in front of her. There were long necks, short necks, hairy necks and pimply necks. Necks with moles, and heads with almost no necks at all.

Her eyes stopped on the neck directly in front of her. It was like a baby's bottom, soft and fuzzy. And how close and unprotected! What if Calliope leaned forward and snapped? The owner of that neck would be enslaved. A blood-sucking zombie who would walk the earth forever. Or at least until Calliope told her she could go home.

Of course, that deliciously pink neck belonged to Noreen, her sometimes best friend. This week was one of those times.

No, Calliope would have to find another victim. Her gaze drifted toward Mrs. Perkins, who stood with her back toward the class, writing a long list of chalky numbers. My, what a large white neck Mrs. Perkins had. And so easy a target. Calliope bet she could reach it in one lunge from her second-row seat.

Calliope softly clicked her fangs and dreamed. She

saw herself leap out of her seat, landing on Mrs. Perkins.

Mrs. Perkins screamed and fought back. Oh, she was a strong one. But Calliope was stronger. Her nails had become claws. She dug into Mrs. Perkins' back, biting her again and again in that fat white neck.

Calliope could taste Mrs. Perkins' blood, and it was sweet. As sweet as getting the last cafeteria doughnut when there was still a long line of kids behind you.

Sweeter yet was the thought of Mrs. Perkins enslaved. Oh, the wicked, wicked things Calliope would make her do. For starters, you could forget tomorrow's math test.

Instead, the class would arrive to the smell of hot fudge. At eight-fifteen in the morning! There'd be a sundae on every desk. One sundae would stand out from the rest. *Big* would be too small a word for it.

And guess whose sundae that was? You got it. Calliope licked the sharp tips of her fangs. For sure, some would complain. And some would learn the wrath of a she-devil crossed. Calliope contemplated the punishments, and that seemed better than the biggest of big sundaes.

She'd hang kids upside down from Velcro wall patches. The boys would have to wear their underwear outside their pants. And for the girls . . .

"*Cal-li-o-pee!*"

Calliope jumped at the sound of her name.

"Calliope!"

"Uh-oh," said Calliope, suddenly realizing that Mrs. Perkins was calling on her. But for what?

"What is ten times ten?" Mrs. Perkins asked in a rising voice.

"Uh . . ." Calliope knew the answer, but she couldn't get it out. Her fangs had somehow locked shut. She flexed her jaw, and *pop!* The fangs flew out, hitting Noreen in the back of the head. Of course it didn't hurt. But Noreen, that stupid crybaby, screamed anyway.

Mrs. Perkins marched over to Noreen's desk and scooped up the wet fangs. She held them out in front of her as if holding a rat by its tail.

"And what, young lady, are these?"

Before Calliope could answer, Mrs. Perkins marched back to her desk. She wrapped the fangs in a tissue and put them in the top drawer.

Calliope's shoulders sank with a heavy thought. She had been defanged by the teacher.

Watch My Head Explode

Calliope hung upside down from a middle bar of the jungle gym. Her red Keds were crossed. Her arms were folded batlike and her thick yellow hair brushed the dirt below.

School was out but Calliope wasn't home. She was still at school, and she didn't like it one bit.

Kids climbed all around her, but Calliope didn't notice. Her white T-shirt hung down, covering her face, which was turning quite red. I'll just hang here until my head explodes, she thought.

You see, Mrs. Perkins had refused to return Calliope's fangs after class. And without her fangs— well, a life without blood-sucking was no life at all.

A bell rang and kids jumped off the jungle gym. They filed back into the school. But not Calliope.

6

She continued to hang upside down, her face growing redder and redder.

Oh, she could hear the other kids clucking now. "Did you hear what happened to Calliope Day?" they'd say in hushed voices. "She hung upside down until her head exploded—and it was all her teacher's fault!"

Calliope's thoughts were interrupted by a loud "Ahem." Startled, she lost her concentration, and her tired legs let go. She dropped to the ground with a thud.

"Playtime's over," announced Mrs. Sterne, the principal. She stood outside the jungle gym and pointed toward the school building. Calliope tried to stand but banged her head on a bar. She crawled out instead, through the dirt.

Mrs. Sterne was waiting for her. She shook her head at Calliope, whose white T-shirt and shorts were now a dusty brown. Calliope's knees were caked in dirt.

"Brush yourself off and get inside to start your homework," said Mrs. Sterne. She headed for the school, waving for Calliope to follow her.

Oh, great, thought Calliope. Time to be a cattle kid.

A what? A cattle kid, a cattle kid, that's what! A cattle kid was what you became after school.

The grown-ups called it the after-school program.

But to Calliope, it felt like a Western—only she and the other kids were the cattle and the teachers were the cowboys. Why couldn't the kids be the cowboys for a change, herding the teachers outside to play? It seemed only fair, to Calliope's way of thinking.

She picked up her backpack, which was sitting outside the door, and walked into the school cafeteria. It was a big room filled with long rows of low tables. Teachers walked among the rows, making sure kids were doing homework and eating their snacks.

"Moooo," Calliope said loudly. She raised her chin, sticking out her lips the way she'd seen cattle do in the movies.

She stood in the doorway for a moment, looking for a good seat. What luck. There was one left near the door. She raced for it, beating out another boy. "Sorry," said Calliope, not meaning it at all.

She stood between her chair and table and looked around. To the left of her was a boy she didn't know. He had a dirt smudge on his cheek and wore a baseball cap backward. "Girl hater," Calliope said to herself.

On her right was Mickey Schmootz. He hunched over a big book, eating cupcakes. The page was covered with chocolate crumbs.

Boy, Mickey sure liked those cupcakes. His bottom barely fit in his small plastic chair. Yep, they'd be coming soon for Mickey. He was ready for slaughter.

8

Okay, okay. So Calliope exaggerated a bit. But her little story about the after-school program was a lot more interesting than the truth. The truth was that they all had to sit around in this big room for the next couple of hours. Then the parents would come home from work and pick them up.

Well, Calliope, for one, just didn't have time for this today. She needed to get home and start plotting how to get her fangs back.

She slammed her backpack onto the wooden table. Mickey didn't look up from his cupcake. But the noise attracted the attention of a passing teacher. She looked sternly at Calliope and motioned for her to sit down.

Calliope lowered herself slowly into the chair, the teacher's eyes following her as she sat. The teacher didn't leave until Calliope's bottom hit the chair. Man, she had to bust out of this joint. But how?

Calliope saw Noreen, her sometimes best friend, enter the cafeteria. The little wheels inside Calliope's head began to spin. Hmmm, she thought. Perhaps there's hope after all.

You see, Noreen loved Twinkies. And those who love Twinkies hate cupcakes. Those who love cupcakes hate Twinkies. And you should never, ever sit Twinkie lovers next to those who adore cupcakes.

Why? Heck, Calliope didn't know. It was just one of those things you picked up after three years in after-school. She used to think all this was stupid. Now she was thankful.

She waved for Noreen to come over. But where would she sit? Don't worry, Calliope had it under control.

She turned toward the girl hater on her left. Calliope smacked her lips together in a loud kiss. Then she put her hand on his knee. "Gee, you're awful cute," she said.

The boy pulled away from Calliope so hard that he fell backward in his chair. He stood up and ran away.

Calliope threw her backpack into the empty seat and waited for Noreen to squirm her way over through the crowd of incoming kids.

"I saved you a seat," said Calliope, removing her backpack.

"Thanks," said Noreen.

Calliope watched as Noreen opened her backpack, taking out a couple of packages of Twinkies and a 7UP. Noreen ripped open the first package, offering a Twinkie to Calliope.

"No thanks," said Calliope. "Mickey says Twinkies are for sissies."

Calliope pointed over her shoulder at Mickey, who was still eating cupcakes. Noreen looked over at Mickey's chocolaty face and fingers. She grimaced.

With her pinkie held high, Noreen raised a Twinkie between her index finger and thumb. She took the tiniest bite Calliope had ever seen. Not a crumb fell.

Calliope turned toward Mickey, whispering in his ear, "Noreen says you're a slob."

Mickey looked up from the cupcake sitting on his book. His mouth was a chocolate ring. "She does?" Mickey said.

Calliope nodded.

Mickey looked over at Noreen. She held her Twinkie high and looked down her nose at Mickey.

"Well, tell her I think she's a stuck-up princess," Mickey said to Calliope. He said it loudly enough so that Noreen could hear him.

"*Hah,*" said Noreen, taking another tiny bite. "At least I know how to eat like a human."

"You're not human," replied Mickey, standing up. "*Humans* don't eat *Twinkies*."

Ooh, Mickey. That was low, really low, thought Calliope, smiling.

Noreen slowly put down her Twinkie, dabbed her mouth with a napkin and then turned to Mickey. "I won't even dignify that with a reply."

With her pinkie held high, Noreen raised her Twinkie again. But she never took the next bite.

Splat! A gob of gooey cupcake hit Noreen in the eye.

No one was more surprised than Mickey. He

stood, mouth open, watching as the cupcake struck Noreen. Where had it come from?

Noreen, of course, had a flair for the dramatic. Remember her little fit in class? She really let loose now. Noreen shot up out of her chair with a scream that rattled the large metal bowls stacked in the back of the cafeteria.

Her hands went to either side of her head. And her Twinkie? Well, the Twinkie went flying. It landed, of all places, in Mickey's open mouth. He gagged as if poisoned, spitting it out.

A spray of chewed-up Twinkie covered Noreen. She reached across the table, scooping up a handful of cupcake off Mickey's book. You know where *that* landed? Right between Mickey's eyes.

The stage set, Calliope climbed on top of the table. She cupped her hands to her mouth and raised the call loud and clear: *"Food fight!"*

The cafeteria exploded in flying food. Teachers rushed for cover. They'd learned to let these things run their course.

Calliope grabbed her backpack and ran out the open back door.

She made a beeline for a row of big trees at the edge of the schoolyard. Once safely hidden behind some branches, she sat down, breathing hard.

She held up a finger stained with chocolate cupcake. She blew on it as if it were a smoking pistol.

The Long
Road Home

Guess what? This was not the first time Calliope had busted out of the after-school program. It was, though, her best escape. Her best escape ever.

She sat against a big tree, catching her breath. How clever she was. Too bad she couldn't tell Mom. But she didn't dare.

It was Mom who had put Calliope in the after-school program. She didn't think Calliope was old enough to stay home alone.

Sure, that was true three years ago, when Calliope was only six. Back then she had never even heard of the after-school program. She thought everyone went home after school, just like she did.

Calliope remembered those afternoons long ago. Her two brothers used to throw her high into the air.

To them she was a human beach ball—and Calliope loved it.

Then Dad got real sick. His death changed everything.

With Dad went indoor picnics on old blankets when it rained on Sundays. Gone too were his big hamburgers with thick slabs of raw onions.

Dad loved onions. He ate them on hot dogs, steak and eggs. Sometimes, when he had nothing to put them on, he'd munch a slice raw.

Dad's breath could make you cry. On school mornings, he'd kiss Calliope's forehead as she slept. She'd awake, her nose stinging from his sweet oniony smell.

Now Calliope had to get herself up. Mom was too busy getting ready for work.

And her brothers? Calliope wouldn't dare ask them to throw her today. They wouldn't stay around to break her fall.

That was okay. Dad had prepared her. "Learn to fend for yourself," he had counseled from his bed. "Live up to your name!"

Calliope's name was Dad's idea. He had named her after an ancient Greek goddess. Calliope, Dad explained, was a Muse, the boss of her eight sister goddesses. She commanded her sisters to write poems and sing songs. And she made them tease and torment the humans.

Oh, sure, Dad. Calliope knew he was making up the last part. She had learned in school that the Muses' job was to inspire humans to greatness, not bug them to death.

Still, she liked Dad's Muses better. And she knew he was fooling around to make a point. The point was this: Be your own girl and don't let anyone push you around.

Yes, Calliope was a special, special name. It was a keepsake her dad had given her and her alone.

"Calliope," she said softly. Her nose twitched with a fleeting sweet oniony sting.

She had sworn to be true to her name. In the past three years, she had taught herself how to get dressed, make her bed and take a shower. She even made her own breakfast: Cheerios with orange juice.

So why, why, why couldn't she stay alone in the house?

"Because you're only nine," Mom said.

"But Mom!"

"But Mom nothing."

Calliope rarely took no for an answer. She argued and argued with Mom about getting out of ASP. That's what Calliope called the after-school program to her mom. Get it? ASP. Like the snake that killed Queen Cleopatra of Egypt.

Finally Mom called a truce. She'd let Calliope

come home at five P.M., an hour before Mom returned from work.

Oh, brother. Did Mom ever mess up. She played right into Calliope's sticky little hands. Mom had given Calliope a rule that she could bend like a licorice stick.

And boy, did Calliope ever bend that rule. She was often home by three. Hey, what self-respecting kid wouldn't do the same?

Besides, it seemed a shame to leave a perfectly wonderful house empty all afternoon. Calliope saw it as her job to fill it up.

Sitting against the tree, Calliope was free of school, but not home free. The trick now was to get home without bumping into anyone Mom knew.

Calliope slithered on her belly through the grass. She headed toward a low, moss-covered stone wall just beyond the trees.

At the wall, she lifted her eyes above the stones. She saw a row of big backyards. They sat behind three-story houses with brightly colored gingerbread trim.

Calliope slithered over the wall and then stood up. She dashed behind a shed. Peering out from behind the shed, she saw a maid in a front window, dusting a lamp.

From the shed, she zigzagged across the backyards. She darted behind a pool chair, crawled to a fence, ran to a plastic slide.

From the slide, Calliope could see a park. Pizza Park, as she called it. Why? Why do you think? Because it was shaped like a slice of pizza. It was black-dirt pizza with a matted grass topping.

Calliope knew Pizza Park well. Her house was just on the other side of it. Pizza Park was busy today. Every rusty swing creaked with a kid she knew.

She could walk around the park, but that took forever. It was much quicker to walk through the park. She decided to chance it.

Calliope imagined herself a drill sergeant. Her red Keds were the men. She drove them hard. One, two, one, two, she counted in her head as she began walking.

Head down, arms swinging and backpack bouncing, Calliope crossed the park in no time. She entered a street of little matchbox houses. They kind of looked like the ones in Monopoly. Only they weren't green and were bigger, of course. But the houses had the same boxy look and were largely identical.

Most of them were white. Each had a neatly trimmed patch of front lawn. The houses were close enough together that some moms leaned out their side kitchen windows, chatting. A few heads turned as Calliope marched by. She didn't look up, hoping

17

no one would recognize her. One, two, one, two, she commanded her feet.

Up ahead there was one house that was different, very different. The front lawn wasn't brown. But neither was it green. There were more blue and yellow flowering weeds than grass.

The house itself was definitely not white. It was purple. But the shutters? That was another story. No one knew for sure what color they were. Some on the street said they were teal. No, others countered, they were aquamarine.

Aquamarine? Not even close. The shutters were turquoise. Calliope knew. She had selected the color herself.

Calliope took the house key out of her backpack and unlocked the front door. She clumped upstairs to her room.

She dropped her backpack in a corner and sat on the bed. Boy, was she tired. Her head drooped for a moment. She looked down at her T-shirt.

What was this? There was a big chocolaty cupcake blotch—and something on it was moving! Calliope looked closer. There were a couple of tiny brown ants crawling around in the blotch. She put her pinkie against the blotch and an ant crawled on.

"Where'd you come from?" Calliope said to the ant, which she had raised to eye level. The ant stood at the tip of her pinkie and waved his antennae at her.

"*Adiós, amigo,*" she said, flinging the ant. She moved her hand to wipe off the blotch but then stopped. What was she doing? She remembered Noreen's face wrinkled in horror. This blotch was a badge, a badge of honor, signifying Calliope's escape from ASP. She wouldn't take off her T-shirt until Mom made her.

She looked about her room. It wasn't much more than a small square box with a little window. Under the window was a low bed. Above the bed were little fluorescent planets stuck to the ceiling.

The room's most distinguishing feature was its shoeboxes. There were dozens of them. They were on her bed, her desk, her bookshelf. Shoeboxes were lined up along the floor.

Each box was piled high with stuff.

Calliope grabbed the shoebox closest to her. It was filled with Barbie heads. Ah, one of her finest collections.

There were redheads, blondes and brunettes. She had heads with black hair, blue hair and even purple hair.

Calliope collected the heads when and wherever she could. Take last Sunday. She had been watching little Sallie across the street and had seen an amazing sight. It was a Barbie with a pageboy haircut.

"Barbies don't have short hair," Calliope had said, holding the Barbie up as though it were a rare gem.

"They do now," Sallie had said, brandishing a pair of scissors.

Poor Sallie. She should never have shown off. For the head of that bobbed Barbie now sat in Calliope's shoebox.

Why, you might ask, did Calliope collect Barbie heads? Because she collected just about anything. You never knew what might come in handy someday. Besides, Barbie heads could be great fun.

Calliope picked up a head and twirled it by the hair. She remembered Halloween. From her bedroom window, she had pelted trick-or-treaters with Barbie heads. Have you ever been hit by a small flying head in the pitch-dark? You should have seen some of the little kids run.

Calliope put down the box of Barbie heads and picked up another. It was filled with greasy plastic insects. They used to be her favorites. Today, though, they were boring!

She put the insects down and grabbed a box filled with all kinds of things. There were a monocle and a pipe sitting on top. Calliope took both. She put the pipe in her mouth and wedged the monocle into her left eye. It was a little big and made her look more like a Cyclops than a detective.

Calliope stood up in front of the mirror over the desk. Hey. She could be the Cyclops detective.

"I say there, Watson," she said, pretending to puff on the pipe. She looked at herself for a minute in the mirror and then popped out the monocle.

"Cyclops detective. That's stupid."

She squatted on the floor and riffled through the boxes under the desk. Rubber bands, shoelaces, magnifying glasses, trading cards and—aha!—Calliope held up a pair of white plastic fangs. She popped them into her mouth and stood up again.

Growling, she looked in the mirror. She snapped twice and turned her head this way and that, examining herself.

Patooey. She spit out the fangs. "It's just not the same."

Yep, her pink fangs were one of a kind. Did you know they had found her—and not the other way around? Really. It's true.

Calliope remembered the afternoon she'd met her fangs. It was just before Halloween and she had not yet decided what she wanted to be. Nothing seemed right.

Then one Saturday, Mom had taken her to a new store. It wasn't in a mall. And you didn't take the highway to get there.

No, Mom had driven on a lot of little streets. It seemed as if she turned every other corner. Calliope

21

was totally lost—and she suspected her mom was, too. Mom got that funny smile she gets when trying to pretend everything was okay.

They finally turned onto a little square, and across the square was a storefront with a sign that said HARRY'S NOVELTIES. What a store! A skeleton hung in the window. The walls were covered with creepy Halloween masks. Little dusty plastic containers were everywhere.

There was one container in the back that immediately caught Calliope's eye. Why? Calliope couldn't say but she was drawn to it like a bee to pollen. She rushed over, plunged in her hand and retrieved a set of pink fangs. See? Those fangs had summoned her.

Calliope popped the fangs in her mouth and it was love at first bite. She didn't even spit them out because they were dusty.

"Now there's a girl who knows what she wants," said the little old man behind the counter. He introduced himself as Harry.

"Hw mch fr the fgs?" mumbled Calliope.

"What?" said Harry.

"Hw mch fr the fgs!"

"How much for the fangs?" repeated Harry.

Calliope nodded vigorously. She decided not to take the fangs out until they were hers.

"Let's see now," said Harry, who seemed to be adding it up in his head. "That's my last set of the pink ones and they're very rare, you know. And they glow in the dark, so that's got to cost you extra."

"Hw mch, hw mch?" Calliope mumbled excitedly.

"All right, I'll tell you what," said Harry. "If you promise to wear them a lot, I'll let you have them for one dollar."

"A dllr?"

"All right, fifty cents, then."

"Fity cnts?"

"You're a tough one all right," said Harry fiercely. "A quarter. And that is my final offer."

Calliope fumbled through her pockets until she found a quarter.

With those pink fangs, Calliope had dreamed up the best story ever. She was a she-devil. It was a Dr.-Jekyll-and-Mr.-Hyde kind of thing, only different. She didn't have to drink anything smelly. And she was always a lovely little girl—except if she opened her mouth. Then watch out!

It was full of sharp teeth. Pink teeth. Teeth that carried venom like a snake.

If bitten, you didn't die. Oh no. That was too easy. If bitten, you were enslaved to Calliope. She imagined kids making her bed. Kids doing her homework. Kids massaging her feet. And yes, kids even brushing her teeth.

Calliope wouldn't bite just anyone. Oh no. You had to be special. Especially naughty, that is. Like

23

the kid who whacked her with spitballs in math. Or Mrs. Brainnot, the science teacher who gave too much homework.

Oh, how she missed those fangs! Calliope looked about her room. The greasy insects, the monocle, the pipe, the magnifying glasses and even the Barbie heads seemed boring now.

She walked downstairs and flopped lengthwise on the living room couch. The springs creaked and her stomach sank lower than the rest of her. The chocolaty blotch on her T-shirt stuck to the frayed fabric.

"Oh, phooey," said Calliope. But she didn't get up.

She rested her head on one hand while the other twisted a lock of yellow hair. She had left the front door open, and a breeze tickled her face.

The house was silent except for the hum of the refrigerator.

"I'm not lonely," Calliope said out loud to herself. "I'm alone. I like being alone."

The refrigerator groaned.

Okay. Okay. So she wasn't crazy about being alone. In the school's crowded cafeteria, she imagined her empty house as something better than it really was.

Besides, what choice did she have? Mom had to work. She couldn't chauffeur Calliope to the mall like some other moms during the school week.

The refrigerator rumbled.

"My, aren't we talkative today?" Calliope said to the refrigerator.

She sat up, a piece of couch tearing off and sticking to her chocolaty stain.

"Okay," she said, pointing at the refrigerator. "You want to know the truth? I'll tell you the truth. There are plenty of kids around. Any of them would be happy to see me. But I don't feel like going visiting, okay?"

The refrigerator went *clunk, clunk, clunk* as its ice maker dropped some new cubes into an inside tray.

"Why?" said Calliope, standing up now and pacing. "I'll tell you why. Because most kids are boring. *B-O-R-I-N-G.* Boring."

Calliope fell back on the couch, arms crossed. She didn't stay angry, though. You want to know why? Because there was somebody who wasn't boring. Well, he really wasn't a somebody.

Meet Mortimer

Calliope raised herself up halfway on the couch and hollered. *"Mortimer, oh, Mortimer."*

Suddenly there was a loud rattling, and then a bang. Calliope heard a clattering sound coming across the kitchen's chipped linoleum floor. And there, stopping where the linoleum met the worn living room carpet, stood Mortimer. He was a huge furry puffball of a rabbit. Mortimer was all white except for a large black patch around one eye.

"Ten seconds, Mortimer," said Calliope, looking down at her large-faced watch. "That's got to be a new record."

Mortimer hopped over to Calliope, who picked him up. She squeezed Mortimer so hard that he popped out of her grasp. He plopped down on the carpet beneath her.

"Mortimer, what a day!" she said. She told him about her great escape and losing her fangs.

"What am I going to do?" she asked Mortimer.

Mortimer didn't answer. He was grazing on the carpet, noisily chewing on frayed carpet ends. Calliope didn't mind. She patted Mortimer's head. She knew he thought best on a full stomach.

Suddenly Mortimer bolted under the couch. Calliope heard the loose board in the vestibule creak. Uh-oh, she thought. That better not be Mom.

Calliope had left the front door open, which was one of Mom's big no-no's. And Mortimer wasn't supposed to be free in the house. No one but Calliope knew that he could get out of his cage.

Calliope looked at her watch. It was only five P.M. Mom wouldn't be home yet. She sat up and turned to face the front door. If not Mom, she thought, who could it be?

Two policemen stood in the vestibule. Yes, policemen. In Calliope's very own vestibule. She sat glued to the couch, studying them.

You know what? These guys were pretty funny-looking for policemen. One was as short as the other was tall. The short one had greasy hair that covered his ears. The other had a crew cut.

In some ways, though, the two were alike. Each of them had a black gun, a belt of silvery bullets and a shoulder radio that crackled like static electricity.

They wore black-and-white name tags. The tall one was Joe, his partner Norbert.

The two officers stood in Calliope's vestibule, wide-eyed and with nostrils twitching. They looked like Mortimer when he was about to run.

"May I help you?" Calliope asked.

The two officers jumped at the sound of her voice. The one named Joe, however, quickly recovered. He stepped into the living room. His partner stayed behind, watching Joe with a nervous smile.

Joe walked toward Calliope. She couldn't take her eyes off his belt. What silvery bullets. Weren't they what you used to kill werewolves? Man, she'd like to have one of those.

The officer stopped in front of Calliope. His head swiveled right and then left as he scanned the living room. He acts like a robot, she thought.

What if these weren't policemen at all? What if they were robots? Alien robots sent to capture her? Hmmm, thought Calliope. Not a bad start for a new game.

Joe's swiveling head came to rest in the middle position. Calliope imagined the top of his head popping open. She pictured a laser rising out of Joe's head and pointing down at her.

Calliope held her breath. For a split second, she really thought she was going to get blasted. Then the feeling passed and she realized that Joe was just staring at her. Well, not at her. At her chocolaty stain. She looked down at it, too. There were still some ants crawling around.

I hope he's not thinking of arresting me for being dirty, thought Calliope. I'm supposed to be dirty. I'm a kid.

Finally Joe spoke. "Is anybody home?"

"I am," said Calliope.

"I mean your mother or father."

Something in Joe's voice made Calliope think she'd better say yes. "Mom's upstairs."

"Would you please get her?" said Joe.

"Okay," said Calliope, rising ever so slowly from the couch. She inched her way toward the stairs. Boy, she'd better think of something quick. Of course Mom wasn't upstairs, but she'd be home soon. Calliope didn't want Mom to catch her here with two policemen. They might tell her that Calliope had been home alone for a while. Could a kid get arrested for being home alone without her mom's permission? She didn't know.

Calliope's nose twitched from a fleeting sweet oniony sting and she thought of her dad. His face popped up in her brain at the strangest moments—but usually for good reason. Calliope heard again his story about her name. "I'll be cleverly naughty," she told herself. Not only would she get rid of these pesky policemen but one of those bullets would be hers, too.

Calliope looked behind her. Neither policeman had followed her upstairs. So far, so good.

Calliope tapped on the door to Mom's room. "Mom, wake up," she whispered. She whispered loudly enough for the policemen to hear her. She tapped and whispered several times.

Then she went into her room, still whispering. "Mom, Mom, get up." As she whispered, Calliope grabbed her shoebox of Barbie heads. She dug through the pile.

"Aha," she said, picking out the one with purple hair. It was one of her most prized possessions. She didn't relish losing the purple-haired head. But it was for a good cause. She put the head in the pocket of her shorts.

She tiptoed back down the stairs. At the bottom, she stopped. "Mom's sleeping," she told Joe, who waited with arms crossed. "She had a headache and took some medicine."

Joe frowned, his eyes again scanning the living room. He sighed and said, "Do you have a rabbit?"

Before Calliope could answer, Joe spotted Mortimer. He was crawling ever so slowly across the living room floor toward the kitchen.

Joe reached down to grab Mortimer, but the rabbit bolted back under the couch.

"Please hand me the rabbit," said Joe.

"Why?" asked Calliope.

Joe stared at her a moment. Then he said, "We've had complaints."

"Complaints?"

"It makes noise. At night," Joe said crisply.

"Really?" said Calliope. Now, this was getting interesting. Calliope had always known Mortimer was not your ordinary rabbit. But she'd never dreamed he had the power to annoy the neighbors. "What kind of noise?"

"I don't know," Joe said crossly. "Just hand me the rabbit."

"I don't know," said Calliope, shaking her head.

"You don't know what?" asked Joe.

"I don't know that I want to."

"Oh, you don't?" Joe said impatiently.

"No, I don't think I do."

"Well then, I'll just get it myself."

Joe knelt and reached under the couch. He called out to his partner, "How about helping me here?"

Norbert reluctantly walked to Joe.

"See if that rabbit is behind the couch," Joe said.

Norbert leaned over Joe, peering behind the couch.

At that moment Calliope rushed forward. She plucked a silvery bullet from Joe's belt.

"Hey!" Joe shouted. He jumped up, knocking over his leaning partner.

Joe reached for Calliope but she scooted halfway up the stairs and out of his reach.

"Gimme that bullet," Joe said.

"Uh-uh," Calliope replied. "But I'll trade you."

She reached into her pocket and withdrew the Barbie head with the purple hair. Grabbing the long hair, she twirled the head. "I'll give you this," she said.

Joe stood frozen, his thumbs hooked into his belt. He glared at the swinging head.

Norbert sat where he had fallen. He looked up at Joe and then at Calliope. His eyes followed the twirling head round and round.

Calliope twirled the head faster and faster as she waited to see if Joe would trade. Suddenly her fingers lost their grip and the head flew into the living room. It hit Joe smack in the forehead.

For a second Joe looked as if he were going to cry. Then he threw up his arms. "I'm a policeman. Not a rabbit catcher," he shouted to no one in particular.

He turned, stomping out of the house. "Why, why, why?" he continued ranting as he left. "Why is it I always get these calls?"

Norbert did not follow his partner. He sat on the

floor, digging through his shirt and pants pockets. Suddenly Norbert beamed. He withdrew a slender metal thing the color of dirty gold.

To Calliope, who still stood halfway up the stairs, the thing looked like a bullet without a head.

Norbert wiggled the headless bullet-thing at Calliope as if it were a worm on a hook.

Calliope frowned, but she couldn't resist. Down the stairs she bounded, clenching the silvery bullet in a fist.

She plopped onto her knees next to Norbert. He offered her the headless bullet and she snatched it out of Norbert's hand.

"It's a bullet shell," said Norbert. He spoke so softly that Calliope had to lean forward to hear him.

"A shell?"

"Yes, from a bullet I fired at practice this morning—see the little dent on the bottom from the gun's hammer?"

Calliope turned the shell upside down and smiled.

"Pretty cool, huh?" said Norbert.

Calliope nodded in agreement.

"I'll trade you this for that," said Norbert, pointing at Calliope's clenched fist.

Calliope raised her fist over her head.

Norbert sighed. "You know you can't keep it."

"Why not?" said Calliope, sinking to her bottom. Norbert, she knew, was right.

"For one, it's not safe," said Norbert. "And two, nice little girls don't take other people's things—and you look like a pretty super little girl."

"Really?"

"Uh-huh."

Calliope lowered her clenched hand and slowly opened it. Inside, the bullet glistened with sweat.

Norbert picked up the bullet.

The vestibule creaked and Norbert and Calliope turned to see Joe standing in the doorway.

"I need that bullet," he growled.

"No problem," said Norbert, standing.

The two policemen walked out the door.

"Wait," called Calliope. "You forgot something." She picked up the purple Barbie head and waved it at the officers from the front porch.

But they didn't look back. With a screech, their car sped off.

"Oh well," said Calliope. She twirled the Barbie head in one hand and in the other held the shell up to the sun. It glistened. "Cool," she whispered. Not a bad trophy for an afternoon's work.

Then she remembered Mortimer. She turned back inside. She dropped to her stomach in front of the couch. "Gotcha," she said as she grabbed Mortimer by his hind legs. Rising to her knees, she held him up to her face.

"What's all this about making noise?" she asked him.

Mortimer twitched his nose and looked away.

"Come on now," said Calliope. "I saved you, re-member? Now you've got to tell me what's going on."

But Mortimer kicked Calliope in the stomach and leaped out of her hands.

Pasta, Anyone?

"**S**paghetti again!" Calliope moaned. "Couldn't we at least have macaroni and cheese?"

Neither Calliope's mother nor her two older brothers answered. Nor did she expect them to. Every night Calliope complained. Every night it was the same: spaghetti, spaghetti, *spaghetti*. Calliope's lament had become a family ritual. She'd moan and then everyone would lower their heads, raise their forks and dig in. Amen.

It was not that Calliope hated spaghetti. She loved it. And she understood that spaghetti was cheap, quick and filling. All she was asking for was macaroni or ravioli every now and then.

But no, Mom was a creature of habit. Once she found something that worked, she stuck with it. And pasta had become her secret for juggling work and weekday family dinners. Lately, though, Mom had begun to change sauces—and Calliope took full credit for that. Except now the sauces had become as predictable as Mom's choice of noodle.

Monday was marinara, with meatballs occasionally thrown in. Tuesday was pesto. Wednesday grated cheese. Thursday clam sauce. On Friday, Mom really cut loose. She opened a jar of each sauce and let you choose.

Although they had a formal dining room (but no dining room table), Calliope's family ate most of their meals in the dinette. The dinette was small, but only if you were big. Calliope fit easily. So did Mortimer, whose cage sat on some wooden crates in a corner between two windows. It gave him a panoramic view of Mom's garden.

Bigger people, like Calliope's brothers and their friends, had a hard time with the dinette. For them sitting down at the table was a delicate balancing act. It required tilting a chair backward enough to slip in. Some of her brothers' bigger friends just couldn't make it work. That was okay with Mom, because then they could never stay for dinner.

As on most weekday nights, the family was huddled around the rectangular table. Calliope surveyed her family. Teenage brother Frederick sat across from her. It was Thursday and he had piled his plate high with spaghetti drowning in clam sauce. Frederick sat hunched over his plate, shoveling in food. His free hand was clenched in a fist alongside the plate.

Calliope reached toward Frederick's plate and he raised his fist to slap away her hand.

"Pig," Calliope said.

Frederick just snorted and went back to shoveling.

Calliope turned to look at her other brother, Jonah. He sat at one end of the table. A philosophy major, Jonah attended Seton Hall University, which was within walking distance. He lived at home.

What was philosophy? Calliope wasn't sure. But it had something to do with asking a lot of questions and getting funny answers.

Jonah too sat hunched over his plate. But he ate dinner noodle by noodle. A spaghetti noodle dangled from his mouth. It creased his thick beard as it inched upward. Jonah's nose twitched each time he loudly sucked the noodle higher.

"Mortimer," Calliope said.

"What?" mumbled Jonah.

"You look just like Mortimer when he eats the carpet."

"Not that stupid rabbit again!" said Frederick. He kicked Mortimer's crate tower, which sat near him.

Calliope stuck out her tongue at Frederick. He tried to stab it with his fork, but Calliope ducked.

Calliope glanced at her mother. She was gazing out the window, twisting her spaghetti tightly around her fork.

"I bet you can't answer this," Calliope challenged Jonah. "Are rabbits as smart as people? Or are people as dumb as rabbits?"

Jonah stopped sucking and cocked his head. A dangling noodle swayed beneath his chin.

"Who cares?" blurted Frederick. His outburst rattled the dinette's windows, silencing everyone.

Calliope decided to listen quietly to the sounds of dinner: Frederick's muffled grinding, the *slurp, slurp, slurp* of Jonah and the thoughtful silence of her mother.

When Calliope felt everyone was good and lost in their own thoughts, she turned toward her mother.

"Mom," Calliope said. "Anyone call after school?"

"I haven't checked with the service, honey. Why?"

"Oh, no reason," said Calliope. "Let me check for you."

Before her mother could object, Calliope was out of her seat. She hurried over to the wall telephone, which hung near the doorway between the kitchen and the dinette.

Calliope felt everyone staring at her as she dialed the family's answering service. "What?" she said, turning to face the dinette.

"Well, you usually let the phone ring and ring—even if you're standing next to it," said Mom.

"I think Calliope's got a boyfriend," said Frederick, smiling wickedly. Jonah nodded.

"A boyfriend?" Mom said. "Good grief, she's only nine."

Calliope stuck her tongue out and concentrated on the recorded messages.

"Mom, your prescription's ready," she called out. Mom nodded.

"Uncle Jerry called."

Then Calliope heard a voice new to her. "Mrs. Day," it rasped. "This is Sergeant Mulcahey, calling about your daughter and her pet rabbit. Would you give me a call down at the station house? 555–6161. Thanks."

Calliope listened to the message again, memorizing the number. Then she smashed the 9 on the telephone, which erased messages.

She looked up to see everyone staring at her.

"Who is it, dear?" her mother asked.

"Oh, uh, wrong number."

That night Calliope lay beneath her covers, pretending to be a worm. She had burrowed to the center of the earth. Only she didn't get burned up by lava. No, Calliope had found a secret chamber. It was dry and not too hot.

This chamber was so deep that no one could hurt Calliope. No matter how hard they stomped. No matter how deep they dug. She would never be fish bait.

But the chamber was a bit too dark, even for a worm. What Calliope needed was a flashlight.

A worm with a flashlight? Hey, this was Calliope's fantasy. She could be a worm in a tuxedo, if she wanted to.

Now, where was she? Oh yes. The flashlight. Every morning as she made her bed, Calliope hid a small flashlight between the pillows and the turned-back sheets. That way the flashlight didn't make a lump. So Mom never noticed it.

Calliope's hand groped under the covers. Aha! There it was. She pulled the flashlight toward her. Next she reached into a pocket in the pants of her pajamas. She withdrew the shell.

She flicked on the flashlight. The shell didn't shine the way the bullet had, but it was still kind of cool.

She reached into her pocket again. This time she withdrew the purple-haired Barbie head. She placed the shell and the Barbie head face to face. She pretended that the shell was Joe the policeman. Calliope, of course, was the Barbie head.

"Hey, you," Calliope whispered, making the shell jump up and down. "Give me that rabbit."

"Yeah, right," snorted the Barbie head.

"I mean it. Give me that rabbit."

"Never," said the Barbie head, and it ran away.

"Come back here," said the shell, chasing the Barbie head.

The two ran in circles.

"Nah, nah, nah," said the Barbie head. "You can't catch me."

"Oh yeah?"

"Yeah!"

The shell leaped at the Barbie head. But it jumped too high and too far. The shell soared over the Barbie head and landed in a nearby pool of lava.

Calliope made a loud sizzling noise and then snickered. "What a dork."

"Calliope!" her mom called from out in the hall. "Are you up in there?"

Calliope froze. She heard her bedroom door creak open. Uh-oh. Mom was checking on her. She flicked off the flashlight and sucked in her breath. Not a muscle moved.

"Calliope," said Mom. "Don't play games with me. It's a school night. Go to sleep."

In a moment Calliope heard the door close. She sighed in relief.

"All right, you," she said, flicking on the flashlight and bearing down on the shell. "I want some answers. Start talking."

44

The shell glistened silently in the light.

"Who sent you?"

The shell glistened silently.

"How'd you know I had a rabbit?"

Still no answer.

"Why do you want Mortimer?"

Calliope put down the flashlight.

"Not talking, eh? We'll see about that."

Calliope picked up the Barbie head. She made the shell run in circles. "No, no, no," it cried out.

"Oh, yes, yes, yes," said Calliope, dragging the shell toward the smiling head with the purple hair. She put the head on the shell.

It screamed and raced around. That stupid shell. It tripped on the long purple hair and fell again into the lava pit.

Oh well, thought Calliope. Looks like I'm going to have to solve this one on my own.

Calliope,
Ace Detective

The next day Calliope stayed in ASP—until she finished her homework, which she did very quickly. Then she slipped out the cafeteria's back door again and ran home.

In the vestibule she dropped her backpack. Snapping her fingers, she called, "Mortimer."

Mortimer's cage rattled. The door popped open and Calliope heard a thud. A moment later Mortimer was at her feet.

"Let's go," she said. "We have a lot of work to do."

The two ran upstairs. In her room, Calliope rummaged through shoeboxes. She picked out a red handkerchief, the monocle and the pipe. In her closet she found a funny plaid hat. It looked like something Sherlock Holmes would wear.

The handkerchief went into Calliope's pocket and the hat went on her head. She put the monocle in her left eye, the pipe in the right corner of her mouth. "How do I look?" she asked Mortimer. He sat in a corner, chewing on carpet ends.

Calliope walked over to her mirror. "It's important to look the part, you know," she said to Mortimer. She studied herself, nodding approvingly.

"Calliope Day," she pronounced, waving the pipe. "Ace detective, master of disguise and protector of rabbits."

"Come on," she called to Mortimer. The two dashed back downstairs to the kitchen.

Calliope picked up the phone and placed the handkerchief over the mouthpiece. She dialed 555–6161. "Sergeant Mulcahey," Calliope said, trying to sound like her mother.

"This is Sergeant Mulcahey," a voice rasped in return.

"Sergeant, this is Mrs. Day."

There was a long pause.

"Mrs. Day?" asked Sergeant Mulcahey.

"Yes, you called, remember?"

"Yes, I remember. You say you're Mrs. Day?"

"Uh, yes," said Calliope, deepening her voice.

"Are you sure?"

"Of course I'm sure," she retorted.

Calliope looked down nervously at Mortimer. He chewed on a shoelace.

"Stop that," she said, shaking her foot.

"What?" said Sergeant Mulcahey.

"Uh, I was just talking to my daughter," Calliope said, shaking her leg. "Calliope! Stop hitting your brother with that frying pan."

Mortimer wouldn't let go of the shoelace. Calliope shook her leg so hard that her monocle fell out. It dropped on Mortimer's head, sending him scampering out of the kitchen.

"Who is this?" asked Sergeant Mulcahey.

"Mrs. Day," said Calliope. "I told you."

"Mrs. Day, eh? It sounds more like Mrs. Day's daughter."

Calliope forced a laugh. "Why, Sergeant. How sweet of you. What a nice thing to say."

Sergeant Mulcahey harrumphed.

"Now, what's all this about my daughter's rabbit?" asked Calliope.

Sergeant Mulcahey didn't answer, and Calliope's heart sank. Then she heard the raspy voice.

"Well, ma'am. Rabbits aren't allowed in the town."

"That's a stupid rule," Calliope blurted out. Then she caught herself. "Uh, I mean, why is that, Sergeant?"

"Rabbits are considered livestock. Livestock and barnyard animals are prohibited."

"But Sergeant," Calliope argued. "Mortimer has never slept in a barn in his life."

"Mortimer?"

"That's my—I mean—my daughter's rabbit."

"I'm sorry. But rabbits are considered livestock and livestock are prohibited. I'm sure you understand."

"I'm sure I don't!" shouted Calliope. She slammed down the phone.

The Midnight Howl

How could she have been so stupid? Calliope lay awake in her bed, staring up at the glowing planets on the ceiling.

In her anger this afternoon, she had forgotten to ask Sergeant Mulcahey the most important question: Who was it who had complained about Mortimer?

Was it Frederick? Surely he hated her rabbit. But he hated the police more. He had never forgiven them for towing away his cherished Mustang, even though it had sat out for months, rusting in front of the house.

How about Jonah? Nah. He barely noticed Mortimer. And surely Mom wouldn't turn in the very rabbit she'd given Calliope. No, it wasn't anybody in her family.

But then who? Who on the street even knew she had a rabbit?

Well, Mortimer did go outside every once in a while. He'd slip out the trap, which was a tiny swinging panel in the bottom of the back door. But Calliope never saw Mortimer go farther than Mom's garden. Actually, it was more like a jungle. Mom had planted all these exotic plants that had grown together into a thick clump of brush. It was hard to see anything back there.

And what if Mortimer had snuck outside the backyard? What damage could he do? The worst Calliope could imagine was Mortimer eating a neighbor's doormat.

Maybe that was the noise the neighbors had complained about. Mortimer's squeal as someone kicked him off a doormat. Calliope giggled at the thought.

Suddenly Calliope heard a sound she'd heard a million times. *Rattle, rattle—bang!*

She looked at the clock. It was one in the morning. She popped out of bed and tiptoed down the stairs. It was pitch-black, so she ran a hand along the wall. In the darkness she heard another familiar sound. A *click-clacking* across the kitchen's linoleum floor.

When she reached Mortimer's cage, the door was open. Behind her, Calliope heard one loud squeak followed by a soft *ooh-eet, ooh-eet.* Mortimer must have gone out the trap in the bottom of the back door. But he'd never used it at night before. At least Calliope had never seen him up this late. Mortimer usually spent the night balled up in the sawdust of his cage.

What gives? thought Calliope. Something was off—and it wasn't just Mortimer. Heck, Mortimer was slightly nuts on a good day.

No, there was something else, something that made her neck feel prickly. Maybe it was standing barefoot in the dark kitchen. Or that funny noise.

She hadn't heard it at first. It was soft and low, but steady. The sound reminded her of a radiator blowing steam. But in the spring, on a warm night?

Maybe somebody had accidentally turned on the heat. Calliope walked over to the radiator in the dinette. She didn't feel the cloud of wet heat that usually shrouded the radiator in the winter.

She knelt, putting her ear against the chipped paint of the radiator. It was still and soundless.

Maybe it wasn't the radiator, but something was definitely hissing. What could it be?

Calliope walked around the kitchen, putting her ear against the refrigerator, the dishwasher and even the microwave oven. All were silent.

In her curiosity about the noise, Calliope had momentarily forgotten about Mortimer. She went to the kitchen door and pressed her face against a pane of

glass. She saw a hunched ball of fur on the back banister.

"Mortimer!" she said.

The rabbit's white fur gleamed in the light of the full moon. His head was cocked back, his tiny teeth bared. Out of that little mouth came the hissing sound.

Weird, thought Calliope. She took a closer look.

Mortimer seemed to be snarling at a stooped figure silhouetted in a second-floor window next door.

"Mrs. Blatherhorn?" Calliope said.

Mrs. Blatherhorn

Calliope sat down on the back steps, holding Mortimer in her lap. He squirmed and snarled at her. What was with Mortimer tonight? He acted as if he were bewitched or something.

"Shhh," Calliope said, stroking back Mortimer's ears. He began to settle down.

Calliope looked up at the silhouetted figure moving around in the window next door. It was a bit late to be puttering about the house, wouldn't you think?

Then again, Calliope didn't know much about Mrs. Blatherhorn. Which, of course, made her wonder. It made her wonder a lot.

Calliope began reviewing everything she knew about Mrs. B. That was what Calliope liked to call her.

Let's see. She was an old lady. She liked to stay

inside. And she looked funny. Well, she did. It wasn't Calliope's fault.

Mrs. B. was tall yet stooped. Her clothes were dark and smelled like the closet. She even had a small wart on the end of her nose. You know what? Calliope suddenly realized. Mrs. B. looked just like a witch!

And you know what else? Calliope thought, growing excited. She acted like one, too.

For starters, she kept this cane. Sure, plenty of old ladies had one. But not like Mrs. B.'s. It was a thick rod of dark wood. The handle was a growling head with windblown hair. It had pointy teeth. Its eyes were deep grooves that seemed to follow you.

Pretty weird, huh? Well, it got weirder. Mrs. B. carried her cane everywhere, but she didn't need it. She walked just fine. Calliope had seen her carry two heavy bags of groceries, one on each arm, the cane dangling from an elbow.

If that cane wasn't for walking, then what was it for? Calliope stroked Mortimer and wondered. Then she remembered a most amazing thing.

It all began when Clarence, the neighborhood newspaper boy, found poor old Deliah Simpson. She had lived across the street from Calliope. No one had seen her in days.

Calliope had thought about letting herself into

Mrs. Simpson's house. She often fed her three cats. But Clarence, that busybody, had beat her to it.

He found Mrs. Simpson's front door unlocked and walked inside. Moments later he came running out, screaming. His cry echoed down the street, and soon every kid on the block was rushing over to Mrs. Simpson's.

Calliope got there first. She had been watching Clarence from her bedroom window. She found Mrs. Simpson sitting upright on her couch. She was as stiff as a board. In one hand she held a moldy glass of Pepsi. The other was outstretched toward the television, gripping a remote.

Well, for nearly a day, nothing was more important on Calliope's street than that remote. It became her street's sword in the stone. Nearly every police officer, dad and teenager (including Frederick) tried to pull it free from Mrs. Simpson. They yanked and they groaned. Someone even tried one of those big locking wrenches with the teeth.

Through it all, Mrs. Simpson sat there grinning, wide-eyed. It was as if she didn't want to be dead. That remote was her last hold on this world.

Mrs. Simpson held on stubbornly.

Then Mrs. B. arrived.

Swinging her cane, she cleared a path through the crowd that had filled Mrs. Simpson's living room.

People stepped aside because they knew the two old women had long been friends.

Mrs. B. stopped in front of Mrs. Simpson. She bent forward, going nose to nose with that frozen face wearing the half smile. No wrinkle or line went unstudied.

"Deliah," Mrs. B. whispered. "Deliah, honey. It's time to let go."

Mrs. B. raised her cane over Mrs. Simpson's head. Then she grabbed the remote. It came free in her hand.

Wow! Was that cool or what? Calliope couldn't stop talking about it—until Frederick threatened to grind her into rabbit pellets. She shut up for Frederick's sake, but she didn't stop thinking about Mrs. B.

Now she looked down at Mortimer. "Have you been bewitched?" she teased him. Calliope laughed. She imagined Mortimer flying, his long ears outstretched as wings.

What if it were true? What if Mrs. B. were a witch? Imagine that. A witch. Living right next door.

Her imagination was on a roll. There was no stopping it now.

If Mrs. B. were a witch, Calliope thought, maybe she could be Calliope's new friend for afternoons. Calliope bet Mrs. B. was full of wonderful stories about magic adventures. Stories that she could make come true.

And don't forget that cane. If they were special friends, Mrs. B. might lend it to Calliope.

Oh, the things Calliope would do! Top of the list was retrieving her fangs. She'd stroll into class, twirling the cane on her arm.

Calliope could hear Mrs. Perkins. "Calliope Day! Give me that cane this instant!"

Calliope would pretend to hand over the cane. But as her teacher reached for it, Calliope would shout out some magic words. Mrs. Perkins would freeze, her arm outstretched. Everyone else in the classroom would freeze too.

Calliope would walk right past Mrs. Perkins, through the class and to the desk at the front of the room. She'd open all the drawers, taking out whatever she wanted. If Mrs. Perkins had any secret stuff, Calliope would find it.

What if Calliope found a love letter from Mr. Riggerio, the gym teacher? He was always talking to Mrs. Perkins in the cafeteria at lunch. Calliope would take that letter, photocopy it and tape a copy in all the girls' rooms in the school.

Calliope snickered at the thought. Oh, she was a wicked girl. The perfect friend for a witch.

Now, where was she? Oh yes. The desk. Well, it would be boring after a while. So Calliope would just get her fangs and stroll out of the classroom. At the door, she would wave her cane. Everyone would unfreeze. But nobody would remember what had happened.

How lovely! Calliope couldn't wait to tell her new special friend about her plan. But first things first. She had to make Mrs. B. like her. That was easier said than done. Calliope didn't know much about witches. But she guessed one didn't tangle with them lightly.

Calliope imagined herself baking a plate of cookies. She'd put on her best dress. The white one with the big purple polka dots.

She'd walk next door after school. Give Mrs. B. the cookies and tell her that her teeth weren't yellow, that Calliope liked black clothes and didn't mind the smell of dirty socks. Then, ever so sweetly, she'd pop the question. Could she, perhaps, just for an hour or so, borrow that beautiful old wooden cane?

Her plan seemed so simple, but . . . one question nagged. Would she be walking into the house of the good witch Glinda or that of the Wicked Witch of the West?

Will You Be My Friend?

Calliope stood hidden behind one of the two tall shrubs that marked the brick walkway in her yard. She wore her backpack. Inside was Mortimer. He squirmed and kicked. "Stop it," Calliope scolded him.

She looked at her wristwatch. It said 3:27 P.M.

Calliope peered out from behind the shrub. Sure enough, there she was. Right on schedule. Mrs. Blatherhorn rounded the corner onto Calliope's street. She pulled a metal cart behind her. In the cart were two cans, a box of tissues and, of course, the cane.

"Here she comes," Calliope whispered excitedly to Mortimer. He stuck his nose out of a small opening in the backpack and sniffed.

For a week, Calliope had timed Mrs. Blatherhorn

from her front window. She rattled by, dragging that pull cart behind her, every weekday at 3:28 P.M.

Calliope pulled back behind the shrub and listened as Mrs. B.'s cart clattered along the uneven sidewalk. Calliope shoved her hands into the pockets of her shorts. In one was a giant M&M's cookie she had baked with Mom.

In the other pocket was a glowing green plastic skull. It had deep-set eyes and a howling mouth with a red tongue. Harry—from the Halloween store— had picked it out himself for Calliope. He said the skull, if rubbed gently, could ward off any evil spell.

Just the same, Calliope wasn't taking any chances. That was why she'd taken Mortimer. A bewitched rabbit might come in handy. Putting the cookie in her mouth for a moment, Calliope reached backward and unzipped her backpack a little more. "Is that better?" she asked Mortimer.

The metallic rattling came closer and closer. Calliope withdrew the cookie. She stepped out from the shrub, blocking the path of Mrs. B., who was dragging her shopping cart up the sidewalk.

Startled, Mrs. B. stopped. Then she recognized Calliope. Mrs. B. spun the trailing cart around to face Calliope and advanced. For a moment it looked as if she was going to mow down Calliope. Then, just as suddenly, Mrs. B. stopped. The cart's wheel nudged Calliope's red sneaker.

Mrs. Blatherhorn and Calliope silently eyed one another. After a moment Calliope swallowed hard and raised her hand with the cookie. "I baked this for you special," she said with a big smile.

Mrs. B. raised her nose and looked down at the cookie. "Would you mind getting out of my way?"

"What's the matter, you don't like M&M's?"

Mrs. B. didn't answer.

"How about peanut butter? I can make peanut butter cookies."

"It's not the cookie I don't like."

Calliope didn't care for the sound of that. She rubbed the green skull in her pocket for protection.

"Now, please," said Mrs. B. "Get out of my way."

Calliope lowered the cookie. "I'm sorry, but I can't."

"I beg your pardon."

"I'm sorry, but I can't," Calliope said again, this time very slowly.

"And why not?" said Mrs. B., her voice rising.

"I want to be your friend."

"You what?"

Boy, Mrs. B. was sure hard of hearing. "I want to be your friend."

"Hah," snorted Mrs. B.

Calliope took that as a no. "Why not?" she asked. "Why not?"

Mrs. B. pointed a gnarled finger at Calliope's house.

"There's that, for starters," Mrs. B. said.

"My house?"

"That's not a house. It's a circus tent."

"What? You don't like the paint job?"

"No, I don't care for the paint job and I don't care for you," said Mrs. B. "Now get out of my way."

Calliope thought she saw smoke coming out of Mrs. B.'s nostrils. She whipped out the green skull, holding it up.

Mrs. B. sighed.

"What happened to all the normal young families that used to live here?"

"We're normal," Calliope said. Mrs. B. stared at her with angry eyes. Was Mrs. B. bewitching her? Calliope raised the skull higher.

Mrs. B. arched her eyebrows.

"Normal? Your family? Hah!"

"What's wrong with us?"

Mrs. B. narrowed her eyes. "Why aren't you in school?" she demanded.

"School's over," Calliope shot back.

"Oh, is it?"

"Well, the classroom stuff is."

"Where's your mom?"

"At work."

"So you're home all alone?"

"Oh no," Calliope said, smiling.

She turned around, revealing Mortimer's protruding head.

Mrs. B.'s nose twitched and she sneezed loudly. She grabbed her cane, waving it wildly. "Get that filthy barnyard animal out of my way," she said.

"It's only Mortimer," Calliope said, ducking.

"Oh, you don't fool me," Mrs. B. wailed. "I know what you're up to. The lot of you! You're trying to run me out of my house. Well, it won't work. Do you hear me? It won't work. I've lived in this neighborhood for sixty years. I'll be gosh-darned if a wild little girl and her smelly barnyard animals are going to run me out. Oh, no sirree."

The cane struck Calliope's hand, knocking her skull to the sidewalk. Mrs. B. pushed past Calliope. Her cart ran over the skull, creasing it with a black tire mark.

Calliope stooped and picked it up. She fingered the tire mark as Mrs. B. rattled up her walkway and into her house.

"This is not good," Calliope sighed.

Mortimer Shows Off

Mrs. Perkins looked into the empty cage she held up.

"Looking for something?" said Calliope, who stood next to her. They were alone in the empty classroom. None of the other kids had yet returned from lunch.

"Where's the rabbit?" asked Mrs. Perkins.

Calliope turned around. Mortimer's head poked up out of the open backpack.

"Have you been carrying that rabbit all morning?"

Calliope nodded.

"Calliope," said Mrs. Perkins.

"Well, he was too heavy to carry in the cage."

"Why didn't you leave him in the classroom?"

"Then my show-and-tell wouldn't be a surprise."

"You always have an answer, don't you?"

Calliope smiled.

"All right then, let's get the rabbit in the cage now," said Mrs. Perkins. She put the cage on a table in front of a semicircle of little desks.

Calliope put Mortimer in his cage as Mrs. Perkins went to retrieve her class from lunch.

The kids streamed in, pointing at the cage as they took their seats.

Mrs. Perkins sat on a high stool behind Calliope and the cage. She clapped her hands three times sharply. The class stopped talking. Every face looked up at her.

"Okay, Calliope, you may begin," said Mrs. Perkins.

"This," said Calliope, pointing to the cage, "is Mortimer."

Calliope paused and sucked in a chestful of air. Then she blew out one long blast: "He's an Angora rabbit. He weighs ten pounds. Mortimer eats carrots, lettuce and radishes. But his favorite food is carpet fuzz."

The class giggled.

Calliope waited for the giggling to stop. Then she announced, "Mortimer can open his own cage."

She withdrew a hunk of frayed carpet from her pocket. "Observe," she said. She waved the carpet in front of the cage, calling, "Mortimer, oh, Mortimer."

The cage began rattling as Mortimer chewed and nudged the metal latch. With a *ping,* the latch opened, and Mortimer leaped at the carpet hunk. He landed in Calliope's arms and she hugged him tight.

The class cheered and clapped.

"What else can he do?" someone called out.

Calliope thought for a moment. "He howls at the moon."

The class laughed.

"Calliope!" Mrs. Perkins whispered sharply from her stool.

"Okay," said Calliope. "It's not exactly a howl. It's more like a whine."

She screwed up her lips, threw back her head and emitted a low but piercing whine.

"Calliope, please," scolded Mrs. Perkins.

Noreen, who sat in a front desk, stood up.

"If Calliope says Morton—"

"Mortimer," Calliope corrected.

"Whatever," Noreen said. "If Calliope says her rabbit can howl—"

"Whine," Calliope interrupted again. She threw back her head and imitated Mortimer.

"If Calliope says her rabbit can whine at the moon, I believe her," said Noreen.

A hand went up in the back row.

"When does he howl, er, whine?" asked a boy named Thomas.

"When the moon's out, stupid," said Calliope.

"Calliope!" Mrs. Perkins barked. She motioned for Calliope to come over.

Calliope turned and walked over to Mrs. Perkins, who leaned down to whisper in her ear. "I know it would be great fun if rabbits could howl—"

"Whine," Calliope interrupted.

Mrs. Perkins' face turned red. "Calliope, everyone knows rabbits are silent."

"That's true—except for Mortimer. He's different."

"Oh, he is?"

"Yep."

"And how so?" asked Mrs. Perkins, more amused now than angry.

"He's bewitched."

"Oh, I see," said Mrs. Perkins.

"Yeah, and I can prove it."

"Oh, you can?" said Mrs. Perkins. "How?"

"Let me bring in Mrs. B. for show-and-tell."

"Who's she?"

"She's the witch."

"The witch?"

"Yes," said Calliope. "You can't have something bewitched without a witch. She's the witch who bewitched Mortimer."

"That makes sense," said Mrs. Perkins, trying not to smile.

Calliope's nose suddenly stung with the sweet smell of onions. Uh-oh. Was she about to think of something dangerously clever? Yes!

"I'll make you a bet," she said.

"Yes?"

"If I prove Mortimer's bewitched, you have to give me back my pink fangs."

"If you can prove Mortimer is bewitched," replied Mrs. Perkins, "I'll *wear* your pink fangs."

Calliope spit into the palm of her hand and held it out to Mrs. Perkins. "Let's shake on it."

Saturday Shopping

"**M**om, do you think Mrs. B. is a witch?"

"Honey, that's not nice."

"Oh no, I don't mean she's crabby."

"You don't?"

"No, I mean a *witch* witch," said Calliope. "You know, with a broom and magic powers."

"I see," said Mom.

Mom and Calliope were talking as they walked through the Pathmark supermarket. Calliope pushed a shopping cart. Her mom walked alongside her, tossing in food. The two smiled at the long rows ahead of them.

It was Saturday morning, Calliope's favorite time of the week. Every Saturday, she and Mom would get up early. Not school early, but early enough. Calliope's brothers would be still asleep.

Calliope and Mom would dress quickly, slip out the back door and jump in the car. They'd drive off singing songs and slapping each other on the thigh.

They were together and alone. No bosses. No boys. No big brothers. No teachers. No hall monitors. No crossing guards (and no policemen, Calliope thought). Just "us two girls," as Mom would say.

Mom grabbed boxes of spaghetti and tossed them into the cart.

"So you think Mrs. Blatherhorn is a witch," said Mom.

"Yeah. Well, I think so. I'm not sure yet."

"What's the evidence?"

"Let's see," said Calliope. "Remember Mrs. Simpson?"

"Yes," Mom said sadly.

"Mrs. B. put a spell on her."

"She did?"

"Yeah. With this cane that is way cool. It looks like it could bite you."

"My goodness," said Mom. "What else?"

"Mrs. B. smells funny, wears dark clothes and has a wart at the end of her nose."

Mom's head nodded at each point Calliope recited.

"And Mom, don't get mad, but she is crabby. Very

crabby. Mrs. B. doesn't like anybody. She doesn't even like Mortimer. She stays inside her house most of the time."

"Hmmm," said Mom. "She sounds lonely and afraid."

Mrs. B., scared? thought Calliope. She didn't look scared the other day. She looked mad. If anyone had been scared, it was Calliope. But only the tiniest bit, mind you.

"Witches don't get scared," said Calliope. "Do they?"

"Well, why not?" said Mom.

Calliope thought about that. "What would she be scared of?"

"Of us, maybe."

"Us?"

"Sure. We're not like her."

Boy, Mom has that right, thought Calliope.

Mrs. B. liked grass. Calliope's family didn't see the point of it. Flowering weeds were prettier and needed less care.

Mrs. B. liked high heels. She wore them on Saturday. She wore them in the supermarket. Everyone in Calliope's family wore sneakers. Even Mom. She had to wear heels at work but changed the moment she was out the door.

And Mrs. B. had no pets, no kids and no friends since Mrs. Simpson died. At least Calliope hadn't seen anybody visit, and she was watching Mrs. B. a lot.

Of course, all Mrs. B.'s friends could be witches. Witches, you know, didn't talk like normal people. No, they each kept a crystal ball hidden somewhere in their house. When one witch wanted to talk with another, she rubbed the ball. You know, like in *The Wizard of Oz*. They didn't need to visit each other in person.

Boy, Calliope would sure like one of those crystal balls. She'd put it on a special stand on the desk in her room. She imagined herself standing over the ball. It would glow as she rubbed it. "Come in, Mrs. B., come in," she'd say. Then Mrs. B.'s face would appear inside the ball.

"Calliope!"

"Huh?" said Calliope. Her imaginary crystal ball vanished and she banged the cart into an open freezer display.

"Sometimes I swear you're only here in body," Mom said with a laugh.

Calliope continued down the aisle.

"Mom, if Mrs. B. is scared, then why is she so mean?"

"Easy," Mom said. "It's a cover."

Calliope looked confused.

Mom explained. "Sometimes, when people are scared, they hide it by being scary."

Calliope looked skeptical.

"Mrs. Blatherhorn fooled you, didn't she?"

What if Mom is right? thought Calliope. She started to feel sorry for Mrs. B. It was Mrs. B. who needed a special friend, even if she was a witch. Yes, Mrs. B. needed someone who was entertaining but thoughtful. Someone who was brave yet kind. Someone who was smart but not stuck up about it. Someone like, well, guess who?

"Well, speaking of the devil," said Mom. "Look who's here."

Calliope caught a flash of Mrs. B.'s black high heels. They turned a corner up ahead. Calliope dashed after them.

Surprise!

Calliope rounded the end of the canned vegetables aisle and skidded to a stop. Ahead, she saw Mrs. B.

Calliope scampered back around the end of the aisle and peered down it.

Mrs. B. held a can of creamed corn in each hand. A pair of low-cut eyeglasses rested on the tip of her nose. Mouthing the words, Mrs. B. read the label of one can. She turned to read the label of the other can. Frowning, she turned back to the first can. Back and forth she went.

Geez, Calliope hadn't known canned corn was so interesting. Maybe it was part of some magic brew Mrs. B. was cooking up at home. Which made Calliope wonder if Mrs. B. had a big black cauldron.

She imagined Mrs. B. in her kitchen. Standing on

tiptoes, she'd peer into a big black pot on the stove. The pot steamed and bubbled.

What did witches eat, anyway? Toad con carne? Candied lizard lips? Creamed corn?

Yuck. Maybe that's why Mrs. B. was so crabby. She needed a decent meal. Her cart never held more than a couple of cans of food. There were two in there now, with a roll of paper towels and, of course, the cane. No wonder Mrs. B. went shopping every day.

Calliope decided to have a little chat with Mrs. B. once they became friends. She would teach Mrs. B. how to buy more than a can of creamed corn.

You know, Calliope considered herself a pretty good cook. Her Rice Krispies Treats were most popular. They stuck to the backs of your teeth.

Calliope imagined a steamy pan of hot Rice Krispies Treats now, and her nose twitched with an oniony sting. Oh yes, she had a wonderful idea. Why not invite Mrs. B. over for an after-school snack?

Calliope grew excited. She quickly thought out a private little party for three: her, Mrs. B. and Mortimer. Calliope was sure Mrs. B. would learn to love him.

What should Calliope make? She decided against the Rice Krispies Treats. This called for something totally awesome. Something like blood milk shakes and caterpillar pie. Wouldn't that impress Mrs. B.!

Oh, don't worry. Calliope wouldn't use real caterpillars. She had this great book that showed how to make creepy food with regular stuff. The blood was red dye and the caterpillars candy.

Okay. What else? Mrs. B. would bring her cane, of course. And why not the crystal ball, too? Yeah. That was it. Calliope even thought up a fun game for them to play.

They'd sit on the living room floor around the crystal ball, eating candy caterpillars. Mrs. B. would rub the ball, calling up some of her witch friends. Then Calliope would say, "Is your fridge running?" If they said yes, Calliope would answer, "Then you better go catch it."

Not bad, huh? How many kids do you know who've made phony phone calls to a witch through a crystal ball?

If the witches got mad, she and Mrs. B. would run upstairs to her room and hide. There Calliope would show off her collection of Barbie heads. She'd even let Mrs. B. pick one out to keep.

And if they were getting along really well, Calliope would show Mrs. B. her bullet shell. No one—except Mortimer, Joe and Norbert—knew she had it. But Mrs. B. could only touch, unless of course she wanted to trade. Calliope would trade the shell for that cane and nothing else.

Okay, everything was set except for one thing. She had to ask Mrs. B. Calliope studied her. She looked harmless enough today, reading the backs of her cans. She had moved on from the creamed corn to the creamed spinach.

What's the worst that could happen? Calliope asked herself. Mrs. B. wouldn't dare turn her into a toad. Not here. Then everyone would know she was a witch.

Calliope took a deep breath and slowly walked down the aisle toward Mrs. B. She stopped right in front of the cart, but Mrs. B. didn't look up. Her eyes stayed focused on the back of a can of creamed spinach.

Calliope stood there for a moment and finally said, "Hello."

Mrs. B. jumped, tossing the can into the air. Calliope ducked as the can sailed overhead and landed with a clunk behind her.

Wow, thought Calliope. Almost creamed by creamed spinach.

"Why, you wretched little girl," said Mrs. B. "Look what you made me do."

Calliope forced a smile. It wasn't easy. Mrs. B. was glaring at her. What was that saying? If looks could kill . . .

This wasn't going at all the way Calliope had imagined. I know, thought Calliope. She turned around and picked up the can of creamed spinach. She stepped toward Mrs. B., offering her the can.

Mrs. B. stepped backward with the cart.

Calliope took another step forward. Mrs. B. backed up again.

Calliope took two steps forward. Mrs. B. backed up two steps.

You know, this is kind of fun, thought Calliope. It was as if she and Mrs. B. were opposing magnets. She wondered whether they'd be drawn together if they were back to back. And she wondered how far—and how fast—she could push Mrs. B. down the aisle.

She walked toward Mrs. B. and Mrs. B. kept walking backward. When Calliope walked faster, Mrs. B. backed up faster. The two raced down the aisle. Heads turned as they passed.

Calliope had never seen anyone run backward so fast. Mrs. B. was pretty good at it. Not once did she lose her footing. Nor did she take her eyes off Calliope. Which, while impressive, may have been a mistake.

Mrs. B. didn't see the tower of cereal boxes behind her at the end of the aisle. Calliope stopped, trying to stop Mrs. B. from backing up more. But Mrs. B. kept going. In fact, Mrs. B. went faster, smiling now as though she'd won.

Crash! Mrs. B. plowed into the tower and disappeared among a shower of boxes.

Calliope dashed off, figuring it was time to rejoin Mom. Behind her, she heard Mrs. B. shouting, "I'll get you—and your little rabbit, too!"

Joe and Norbert Return

"**D**on't be afraid, Mortimer." Calliope held him upright around the middle as she lay on her living room couch. His little feet rested on Calliope's belly. "Mrs. B. didn't mean it." Did she? wondered Calliope.

Calliope put Mortimer's little front paws over his head, which she moved slowly back and forth.

"There, there," said Calliope. "Didn't I come home early from ASP? I'd never let anyone hurt you."

Suddenly the vestibule creaked. At the sound, Mortimer kicked and squirmed. "Ouch," said Calliope, dropping him. He leaped off the couch. *Thump,* he hit the floor and flattened himself against the carpet. He looked up at the open front door. What he saw made him run under the couch.

Joe and Norbert were back.

This time Calliope was ready for the policemen. She jumped up and, with legs spread and arms crossed, planted herself in the middle of the living room. "You can't have Mortimer," she told the policemen.

The officers said nothing. They entered the living room. Silently Joe and Norbert circled Calliope. They peered into the kitchen, into the dining room and up the stairs. Finally they stopped in front of Calliope. Norbert looked at Joe, who nodded.

"Is your mother home?" whispered Norbert.

Calliope couldn't understand him. She cupped a hand to her ear and boomed, "What?"

Norbert looked at Joe, who said, "He wants to know if your mother is home."

"Tell him no," said Calliope.

Joe turned to Norbert, opened his mouth to speak and then stopped. He glared at Calliope.

Joe poked Norbert in the ribs with his nightstick and nodded at Calliope. "All right, all right," whined Norbert, slapping away the nightstick.

"Are your brothers home?" Norbert asked slightly more loudly.

"Nope," said Calliope.

Norbert paused. He drew in a big breath. "So you're home *all alone*?"

Calliope cocked her head, examining the short policeman. Oh, for her fangs! What vengeance she would wreak. Norbert's thick neck would taste good. For now, though, she said, "Yep."

Her answer left Norbert speechless. Joe, however, was whispering, hard. "Go on, go on!"

Finally Norbert spoke. "Will you—I mean—could you—I mean—you'll have to come with us."

Calliope thought about that for a moment and her nose filled with the smell of onions. "You mean I'm under arrest?" she asked.

"No, of course not," said Norbert.

"Then why do I have to go with you?" Calliope asked.

Norbert looked at Joe, who said, "Because we said so."

"So I *am* under arrest!" Calliope said gleefully.

"No, you're not under arrest," said Norbert.

"Then I'm not going with you."

Norbert looked panicked. "Okay. Okay. You're under arrest."

Calliope didn't move, though. Instead, she thrust out her arms.

"Cuff me."

"What?" said Norbert.

"I think she wants you to handcuff her," said Joe.

Norbert turned white.

"If I'm under arrest, then you have to handcuff me," said Calliope. "What if I try to escape?"

"I never thought of that," said Norbert.

85

"She's not going to escape," sputtered Joe. "She's not even under arrest."

"Oh yes I am," said Calliope, stomping her feet. "Norbert said so, didn't you?"

"All right, that's it," said Joe. "You want to be under arrest?" Joe grabbed Calliope's little white wrists in his big meaty hands and snapped on handcuffs. "There. Happy now?"

"Gee, thanks," said Calliope. She tried to hold up the handcuffs, but they slid down her arms.

Together the three marched out of the house. Calliope walked between the two policemen. She rattled her handcuffs like chains. "I am the ghost of Christmas past," she moaned.

"Knock it off," barked Joe as he opened the back door of the patrol car. Calliope slid into the backseat. She rattled her handcuffs at Joe, who slammed the door.

He got behind the steering wheel and Norbert sat beside him.

Calliope saw Joe looking at her in the rearview mirror. She stuck out her tongue at him. Then she loudly rattled her handcuffs at him. "Oooh," she moaned.

"Oh, brother," sighed Joe. He started up the car and floored it. Calliope was thrown against the backseat. Her head turned to face the side window. She saw Mrs. B. peering out from behind a foyer curtain.

The Pillsbury Police Boy

Cuffed hands held high, Calliope marched proudly between the two officers into the police station. It was a crowded, busy place. There were people scurrying this way and that.

But one by one, all the people stopped as they noticed Calliope. She rattled her handcuffs and moaned.

"Stop that," scolded Joe.

Calliope stuck out her tongue at him again. She heard some snickering nearby and puffed out her chest.

Suddenly a huge man—he looked like the Pillsbury Doughboy stuffed into a blue uniform—stepped in front of the trio. He boomed, "What in the Sam Hill is going on here?"

The two officers stopped and each turned as white

as a sheet. Norbert tried to uncuff Calliope, but she yanked her hands out of his reach.

"I'm under arrest!" she said, beaming.

"You are?" growled the Pillsbury policeman. He glared at the two officers. "The three of you. In my office. Now!" he barked.

The office was small and cramped. Most of it was filled by a giant wooden desk. On the desk was a little sign that said CHIEF. The huge man sat down behind the placard.

He motioned for Calliope to sit in a wobbly folding chair in front of his desk. Norbert and Joe stood behind her, staring at their feet.

Calliope wedged her handcuffed hands between her legs. She didn't want anyone trying to uncuff her again.

Calliope looked up at the Pillsbury policeman. He leaned back in his chair. His huge belly rose up above the desk. That belly wasn't quite covered by his shirt. Calliope could see half of a hairy belly button. She giggled and then wondered what would be the polite thing to do. Should she point out to the Pillsbury policeman that his belly button was sticking out? Or just ignore it? She decided to ignore it, although that was hard. That big hairy belly button stared at her like an evil eye.

She decided to change the subject. "Where's the hot lights?" she asked.

"Huh?" the chief said.

"Aren't you going to interrogate me, ask me all sorts of questions?"

"Of course not," the chief said, glaring up at the two standing officers. "Don't you know why you're here?"

"I'm under arrest."

"No, you're not under arrest."

"I'm not?" said Calliope, slumping in her chair.

"No, you're here for your own protection."

"From what?"

"Were you home alone?"

"Yes."

"In my town, a little girl is not supposed to be home all alone."

"Why not?"

"Something might happen."

"Like what?"

The chief paused, his pasty face reddening.

"Well, what if a stranger came into your house?"

"You mean like those two?" said Calliope, pointing at Norbert and Joe.

"Yes— No, that's not what I meant," the chief said, pounding the desk with his fist. "Look," he said, standing. "You can't stay in your house alone. It's against the law."

"It's against the law to be in my own house?"

"It is if you're under sixteen. You need adult supervision." The chief picked up the telephone on his desk. "What's your mother's work number?"

"Uh . . ." Calliope felt the wheels of her brain spinning fast. "It's 555–2929."

The chief dialed the number. "May I speak with Mrs. Day?"

Calliope heard the faint sound of what sounded like Chinese coming from the telephone.

"What?" said the chief, holding the phone out from his head. He glared at Calliope.

She shrugged. "Mom does the books for a Chinese restaurant. She's the only one who speaks English."

Calliope's story was half true. Mom was an accountant. But the number Calliope had given the chief was that of her family's favorite Chinese take-out restaurant. No one spoke English there except a teenage son. He usually didn't arrive at the restaurant until about five, when he manned the telephone as the takeout orders started coming in.

"I have an idea," Calliope said. "Why don't you just take me over to Mrs. B.'s? I can wait there until Mom comes home."

"Mrs. B.?" grunted the chief.

"You know, Mrs. Blatherhorn."

The chief's forehead wrinkled at the sound of Mrs. B.'s name. He looked at the two policemen and motioned for them to follow him out of his little office.

The three huddled, heads bent. The chief whispered and pointed a fat finger in the officers' faces.

Calliope poked her head outside the office. "Can I go to my cell now?" she asked sweetly.

The chief ignored her.

Fine, be that way, thought Calliope. Cuffs held high, she walked over to the chief's desk. It was covered with paper. Nothing much interesting there.

Calliope carefully lowered her hands and started opening drawers. There were pencils and more paper. In the bottom drawer, though, she did find something interesting. There was a nightstick, a blue police cap and a big black whistle.

Calliope let the handcuffs slide to the floor. She put on the cap, which sank low on her face. Then she picked up the nightstick and whistle.

Underneath was something that really caught her eye. It was a yellow pad. On it was written MRS. BLATHERHORN. The name was in capital letters and underlined.

Calliope put down the nightstick and whistle. She picked up the pad and looked closer. Under Mrs. B.'s name was a lot of scribbling. Calliope couldn't read most of it. But a few words were clear. There was *alone* and *home* and *school*.

In the middle, as clear as could be, was Calliope's name.

Calliope put down the pad. Her nose twitched with that oniony sting and she picked up the nightstick and black whistle. Sauntering out of the office, she twirled the nightstick. The chief and the officers were arguing and didn't see her coming. She stopped behind the chief. She slapped the back of his leg with the nightstick and blew the whistle as hard as she could.

The chief shrieked and jumped into the air. He landed with a thud that shook the building.

Calliope looked down at the shaken man at her feet and said, "Okay, buddy, let's move it along there."

Calliope Pays a Visit to Mrs. B.

Oh well. Free again. But that was okay. Jail had been a bust. Calliope had never been interrogated, never been given bad food, never been put in leg irons. She'd never even got to see her cell.

Instead, she found herself again riding in Joe and Norbert's patrol car. She slumped in the backseat, looking through a little barred window at the backs of the officers' heads.

The car turned onto Calliope's street. "Hey, I've got an idea," she said, suddenly sitting up. "How about some ice cream?"

Joe and Norbert didn't reply.

"You guys ever have a brown cow?" Calliope rubbed her stomach and smacked her lips. "I can see it now. Thick brown foam bubbling over the top of a tall glass."

Calliope pressed her face against the barred window. "Yes, and a big scoop of vanilla ice cream bobbing in the soda. Root beer or Coca-Cola—your choice."

Joe stared, expressionless, straight ahead.

"You guys are no fun," said Calliope, folding her arms and falling back against her seat.

She looked out the window. The car drove past her house. "Hey," she said, pointing at her passing home.

The car stopped at the house next door.

"You *are* taking me to Mrs. B.'s," said Calliope, shaking two clenched fists. "Yes!"

Norbert turned around to look at Calliope. "You really *want* to come here?"

"Mrs. B. and I are best friends," said Calliope.

"I find that hard to believe," said Norbert.

"Why, because she's a witch?"

"She's a witch, all right," said Norbert, chuckling.

"Not all witches are bad, you know," said Calliope. If only Mrs. B. could hear her. She'd see what a good friend Calliope was.

"All right, you two," Joe said. He looked at Norbert and then pointed at Mrs. B.'s house. "Go knock on the door and see if she's home."

"Not me," said Norbert. "Didn't you hear? She's a witch."

"Very funny," said Joe.

"I'll go," said Calliope. She bolted out of the car.

"Hey," Joe called after her.

But Calliope didn't stop. She bounded up Mrs. B.'s front steps. She rang the doorbell. No one answered. She grabbed the doorknob. It turned, and the door opened.

"Oh, look, it's unlocked," Calliope called out to Joe and Norbert. They still sat in the patrol car. Both of them stared, mouths open, as Calliope disappeared into the house.

Inside, she found herself in a dim foyer. The only light was the late-afternoon sun, which shone through the door's side glass panes. In front of her was a carpeted staircase.

There, lying at the bottom of the stairs, was the cane. Its snarling head stared up at Calliope. She felt those deeply grooved eyes challenging her. *Go ahead. Pick me up—if you dare.*

Oh, she dared. Who did this cane think it was dealing with?

Calliope grabbed the cane and twirled it once above her head—just to show it who was boss. Then she slowly lowered the cane and looked it in the eye. "Now, where's your master, hmmm?"

Calliope could have sworn she saw the cane's

left eye drift ever so slightly toward the stairs. She looked too. For the first time, she noticed a faint trail of handprints leading up the carpeted stairway. "Aha!" Waving the cane, she bounded upstairs.

The Hunt
for Mrs. B.

At the top of the stairs, the trail of handprints dissolved into a mess of scuffed carpet.
"Hmmm."

Behind her, Calliope heard the front door open.
Joe and Norbert stepped into the foyer. "I don't
think Mrs. Blatherhorn's home," said Norbert.

"Shhh," Calliope said loudly from the top of the
stairs. "I'm trying to think." She scanned the upstairs hallway. It was dark and musty. There were
three doors. All but one were open. Calliope raised
the cane's snarling head to her face. "What do you
think?" she asked. She put the head against her ear.
"Me too," she said. She headed toward the closed
door.

"Mrs. B.?" she called softly. No one answered. Calliope knelt and peered through the keyhole. There

was a low bed and a nightstand with a clock radio, but no Mrs. B.

"Here, you try," Calliope said, putting the eye of the cane against the keyhole. She slowly turned the cane. "See anything?

"Nah, I didn't think so," she said, standing up. "I say we go in."

Calliope grabbed the doorknob, turning it slowly. The door opened with a moan.

Mrs. B.'s bedroom was bigger than it looked through the keyhole. The bed and nightstand were in front of Calliope. But there was another half room to the left of the bed. It had a small table and chairs. The furniture sat in front of a fireplace.

And to the right was a closet the length of the wall. It had a sliding door, which was open a crack. Sticking out of the crack was the faintest wisp of gray hair.

Calliope raised the cane to her face and pointed at the closet. "Shhh," she said, putting a finger to her lips.

Oh, that Mrs. B. How she loved playing hard to get. Well, Calliope liked to play too.

"I know," Calliope whispered into the cane's ear. "Let's see if we can't make Mrs. B. come out."

Now, what would drive Calliope crazy enough to come out of the closet? Why, someone messing with her stuff, of course.

Calliope tiptoed over to the bed. With the cane held high in both hands, she jumped as hard as she could on top of the mattress. Hey, not bad. The bed was a bit stiff but still very bouncy.

Up and down, up and down, Calliope bounced. She kept one eye on the wisp of gray hair. It didn't move.

Still bouncing, Calliope let go of the cane with one hand and reached over to hit the On button of the clock radio. It played Brahms' Lullaby.

Very nice, thought Calliope. But not what she was looking for. She ran a finger along the tuning dial. She didn't stop until the radio blared with the driving sound of electric guitars.

The music hurt even Calliope's ears. She turned, smiling, toward the closet. But the gray hair didn't seem to mind. It just hung there.

Hmmm, thought Calliope. Maybe Mrs. B. had turned herself to stone. Witches can do that, you know. They can also step out of their bodies as if they were a pair of shoes. Then their spirits are free to cruise the universe.

Either way, it didn't make a difference to Calliope. She wasn't giving up. Mrs. B. just had to come out.

Calliope turned the clock radio off, on, off, on.

"What's going on up there?" Joe called up the

stairs. Calliope didn't answer. She cranked up the radio and furiously turned it on and off. The hair didn't move.

Soon, though, the radio bored her. She stopped bouncing. Her bottom was getting sore.

She laid the cane across her lap and opened a little drawer in the nightstand. Inside was a writing pad. She took it out, glancing back at the closet.

The pad had a list on it. The handwriting was tiny but precise. It was easy to read. What Calliope read was a list of names. Next to each name was a telephone number, a date and a check mark.

The first name on the list was Sergeant Mulcahey. Calliope touched the date next to the sergeant's name. Wasn't it the day before Joe and Norbert had first come to her house?

Under the sergeant's name was the police chief's.

Calliope heard a *clomp, clomp, clomp* of heavy shoes coming up the stairs. "What's going on up there?" Joe called again.

Calliope stuffed the pad back in the drawer and jumped off the bed. She marched over to the closet. Putting the cane under one arm, she grabbed the closet door with both hands. She grunted as she tugged on the door. The crack widened a little with each tug.

In a moment the crack was wide enough for Calliope to fit her face through. She peered down into the darkness. At her feet she saw what looked like a scrunched-up ball of Mrs. B.'s clothing.

The ball looked up, snarling.

"Why, Mrs. B.," said Calliope. "It's you!"

Mrs. B. bared her teeth. My, if she didn't look just like the face on her cane!

Calliope offered her hand to Mrs. B., but the old woman slapped it away.

Just then Joe and Norbert entered the room. They came up behind Calliope. Norbert peered over her shoulder into the closet.

"Mrs. Blatherhorn?" he said.

"Oh, she's in there, all right," said Calliope. "But she's kind of cranky."

"I am not!" huffed Mrs. Blatherhorn.

Oh yes you are! Calliope thought. But no matter. Calliope had a wonderful idea. She'd figured out how to get Mrs. B. out of the closet.

Why not float her up and out? Yes, Calliope would put that magic cane to work.

"Stand back," said Calliope. She raised the cane in both hands over her head. Joe and Norbert took one look at it and stepped back.

"Rise, rise up," chanted Calliope.

Mrs. Blatherhorn glared up at Calliope. "That's my cane! Give it to me this instant."

Calliope shook her head. This time she closed her

eyes. She imagined Mrs. B. rising out of the closet and floating over the bed. In her mind, Calliope let Mrs. B. drop with a thud. She giggled at the picture but then grew serious again.

With her eyes still closed, Calliope raised herself up on her tiptoes. She held the cane as high as she could. "Rise, rise up!" she boomed.

She opened one eye, peering into the closet. "Darn." Mrs. B. still sat balled up in the closet, glaring at her.

Calliope let her arms drop. The head of the cane banged the floor. Two bony hands shot out of the closet and grabbed the bottom of the cane. "Aha!" boomed a triumphant Mrs. Blatherhorn.

Instinctively Calliope pulled back. She spread her legs and braced her arms. Back and forth, the two yanked and pulled.

Boy, Calliope thought, Mrs. B. sure is strong. Especially for an old lady. No way was she going to win, though. Calliope considered herself a tug-of-war champion. Her fourth-grade team had pulled down boys bigger than Mrs. B.

"Give up?" said Calliope.

"Never," replied Mrs. B., hands red from pulling. Every muscle in her frail arms bulged. Her hair had become a halo of gray wisps.

Okay, thought Calliope, you asked for it. She sucked in her stomach and fell backward.

Mrs. Blatherhorn came flying out of the closet, landing on top of Calliope.

The two officers rushed over. Joe lifted Mrs. Blatherhorn off Calliope. "I've got it, I've got it," chortled Mrs. Blatherhorn, waving her cane.

Joe held her wriggling body out and away from himself. "Put me down, you oaf," barked Mrs. Blatherhorn. She whacked Joe's hand with her cane. He let go and Mrs. Blatherhorn hit the floor and crumpled. She lay still in a heap.

"Joe, you've killed her!" shouted Norbert.

"Oh, fiddlesticks," said the heap. "Help me up."

Joe extended his hand, pulling Mrs. Blatherhorn to her feet. Once standing, she looked Joe up and down. "Burglar," she snorted.

Joe opened his mouth to speak, but Mrs. Blatherhorn cut him off.

"How dare you let yourself into my house?" she said, shaking her cane in his face.

"I can explain," chirped Calliope, who had by now picked herself up off the floor.

All heads turned to Calliope.

"You see, someone tattled on my mom. Although she didn't really do anything wrong. She left me home alone, which is okay. I'm home alone every afternoon and I do just fine. Anyway, the police—after arresting and handcuffing me—took me to jail."

Mrs. Blatherhorn looked in horror at the officers, who stared at their shoes. "I didn't tell you to arrest her!"

"We didn't," insisted Joe.

"Oh yes they did," said Calliope. "And they'll lock me up for the rest of the day—unless, of course, I can stay with you."

"Just until her mother gets home," pleaded Joe.

"Well, I never," said Mrs. Blatherhorn.

"If you don't take her," Norbert said, "we'll have to keep her at the station—and that's no place for her."

"Pleeeeze," said Calliope.

Mrs. Blatherhorn's face reddened. She mumbled something.

"What?" said Calliope.

"I said *all right*!"

There's an Ant Up Your Nose

No sooner had Mrs. Blatherhorn consented than the officers vanished. Mrs. Blatherhorn and Calliope stood alone in the small bedroom. They eyed each other silently.

Finally Calliope slipped her hand into Mrs. B.'s. "I have an idea," she said. "How would you like to meet Mortimer?"

"No thanks," said Mrs. Blatherhorn, withdrawing her hand. "We've already met."

"Oh, that's right," said Calliope, remembering the encounter out in front of her house.

"All right, we'll stay here." Calliope marched over to the table and sat down in one of the chairs. It felt as if she were sitting on a wooden board and the stiff chair didn't fit her body. Squirming, she looked about.

For the first time, she noticed a large oil portrait hanging over the mantel behind her. It showed a big man in a charcoal-gray suit. He had a white handkerchief neatly folded in his breast pocket. He sat in a wooden chair not unlike Calliope's. His legs were crossed and he looked down his long nose at Calliope.

"Who's that?" said Calliope.

"That," said Mrs. Blatherhorn, "was the late Mr. Blatherhorn."

"Late? For what?"

"No, dear, he passed away."

"You mean he's dead?"

Calliope's nose twitched for a moment with the sharp smell of raw onion. Her eyes watered.

"Did he die all of a sudden?"

"Oh no," said Mrs. B., walking over to Calliope. "He lived a long life and died peacefully in bed."

"Sounds nice," said Calliope.

"Nice!" said Mrs. Blatherhorn.

"Yes," explained Calliope. "My dad died in a hospital. He had all these tubes going in and out of him. I wanted to rip them out and take him home. But I never got the chance."

Mrs. B. leaned on her cane, gazing at Calliope.

Calliope looked back up at the painting. "No one ever painted a picture of my dad."

"Well," said Mrs. B., "Mr. Blatherhorn was a judge, and the mayor for a while."

Calliope nodded respectfully. "But did he ever smile?"

Mrs. B. looked up at her husband's sour face. "Uh . . . well."

"I thought not," said Calliope. "My dad smiled all the time. Just like this, see?" Calliope grinned a grin that beamed like the headlights of an oncoming car. Most people froze like a deer when Calliope flashed this smile.

But not Mrs. B. Her thin lips began to stretch. They stretched and stretched until her teeth showed and her cheeks wrinkled.

If this is a smile, thought Calliope, it sure looks like it hurts.

Mrs. B. and Calliope beamed at each other silently. Then Mrs. B. narrowed her eyes and asked, "Would you like some tea and cookies?"

Now, normally Calliope would have quickly answered yes. But there was something about the way Mrs. B. asked that made her pause. It sounded more like a challenge than a question.

Still, cookies were cookies. "Why, I'd love some," said Calliope.

Mrs. B. disappeared. Calliope jumped out of the chair. She bounced once on the bed and turned the clock radio on and off. Then she sat at the table again. She looked up at Mrs. B.'s husband. "What are you staring at?" she said, sticking out her tongue at him.

Mrs. B. reappeared at the door. With one hand, she carried a silver tray. It held a plate piled high with cookies, a flowered teapot, milk and two cups and saucers. Her cane dangled from the crook of the arm that held the tray.

Calliope marveled at Mrs. B. Erect and smiling, she lowered herself ever so lightly into the chair across from Calliope. Mrs. B. looked at Calliope with a challenging smile that said *See if I jiggle a single glass*—and she didn't!

"Let's have a tea party," said Mrs. Blatherhorn.

A tea party? thought Calliope. You mean like Alice and the Mad Hatter? Yes, things were getting curiouser and curiouser. Why was Mrs. B. being so nice all of a sudden? Was it part of some evil spell, or was she a good witch after all?

"I'd love to," Calliope said.

"Cookie?" said Mrs. Blatherhorn, offering the plate to Calliope.

"Why, thank you."

Calliope picked a cookie and inspected it. Looked okay. She sniffed the melted top of an M&M. Smelled like chocolate. She took a little bite. Hmmm, very sugary. Calliope pushed the whole cookie into her mouth. She scooped up a handful of others and began to eat them hungrily.

"Now, may I ask you a question?" said Mrs. Blatherhorn.

"Of course," mumbled Calliope, her mouth still full of cookie.

Calliope didn't know what Mrs. B. was going to ask. All she knew was that she probably wasn't going to like it. She slapped her hands together to shake off the cookie crumbs. Then she grabbed her teacup with both hands and took a big gulp.

"Do you like being left alone?" asked Mrs. Blatherhorn.

"I'm not alone."

"You're not?" said Mrs. Blatherhorn, raising an eyebrow.

"Of course not. Remember? Mortimer?"

"Oh yes, him."

Calliope leaned forward. "Actually, between you and me, I'm not really sure if Mortimer is a him. I just like the name."

"I see," said Mrs. Blatherhorn. She lifted her teacup by its thin handle, holding it between her index finger and thumb. Mrs. Blatherhorn's pinkie pointed at Calliope as she sipped her tea. She put down the cup and pressed on.

"I'm sorry your dad passed away. Really. I am. But shouldn't your mother's first responsibility be to you?"

"You mean Mom should stay home from work?"

"Exactly!"

Calliope tried to picture Mom not working. It wasn't a pretty sight. There'd be no more lying around on the couch with Mortimer, that was for sure. No, Mom would put her to work. Calliope imagined herself polishing the furniture or vacuuming the living room. Yep, Calliope liked things just as they were.

"No thank you," Calliope said politely, but she could see her answer wasn't the right one. Mrs. B.'s scalp reddened under her thin gray hair.

Calliope knew that look. She'd seen it on Mom a million times. It meant something was about to blow. At times like this it was best to keep quiet—and that's what she did.

She watched Mrs. B. fumble with the cookies. Mrs. B. couldn't find one to her liking. Finally, digging to the bottom of the pile, she settled on a big cookie with lots of M&M's.

There was something curious about that cookie. Calliope stared at it until her eyes felt as if they were going to pop out.

Could it be? It was! There was a tiny brown ant circling on the cookie, which Mrs. B. held between her thumb and index finger.

Calliope stopped chewing. She glanced down at the cookies on her plate, turning them this way and that. No ants. She stuck an index finger into her mouth and fished around. If there had been any ants before, they were mush now.

Mrs. Blatherhorn watched Calliope with a grimace.

"Sorry," Calliope said, taking the finger out of her mouth.

Mrs. Blatherhorn raised her cookie and bit. She missed the ant, but it crawled onto her lip. Soon it was racing around her cheek.

For once Calliope was speechless. She'd never seen anything like this. That ant was racing all over Mrs. B.'s face and Mrs. B. didn't seem to feel a thing. At least not enough to stop talking. She just blabbed and blabbed. "Let's go back to the police station. Let's ask the police to make your mom stay home. Wouldn't that be nice? Having your mom around all the time?"

Calliope tuned out Mrs. B. and gave her full attention to that darn ant. Around and around it ran. Finally it went up Mrs. B.'s nose.

At that moment Mrs B. leaned forward, smiling. "Let's go to the police station, just you and me. What do you say?"

Calliope considered the proposal for a moment and then replied, "You have an ant up your nose."

"What?"

"I said you have an ant up your nose."

Suddenly Mrs. B.'s nose twitched. Then it

twitched again and again and again. Mrs. B. wrinkled up her nose until Calliope could see up both nostrils. In the left one, the ant hung from a gray nose hair.

Mrs. B.'s eyes crossed as she tried to look down at the ant. She swung at her nose. Her hand hit it so hard that she knocked herself backward onto the floor.

"Let me help," said Calliope. She leaped out of her chair, landing on top of Mrs. B., and stuck a finger up each of Mrs. B.'s nostrils, fishing around for the ant.

"No, no, no!" screeched Mrs. B. She slapped away Calliope's hands and rolled out from under her. Now she lay next to Calliope, spinning in circles. "Get it out, get it out!" Mrs. B. cried.

Lying on her belly, Calliope watched Mrs. B. go round and round. It made her head dizzy. Then she had an idea. She jumped up and dashed out.

Moments later she was in her own kitchen. *"Aha,"* she said, grabbing the Dustbuster off its holder next to the refrigerator. She ran back to Mrs. B.'s house and up to the bedroom.

Mrs. B. still writhed on the floor. Calliope held up the Dustbuster.

Mrs. Blatherhorn stopped spinning and looked up at Calliope. Her face blanched as she watched Calliope approach. Calliope held the Dustbuster out in

front of her, revving it like a hot rod. Mrs. Blatherhorn stood up and fled.

Calliope chased her.

"Don't be afraid, Mrs. Blatherhorn," Calliope said. "I'll suck out that ant."

But Mrs. Blatherhorn didn't stop. She ran downstairs and out the front door.

Mrs. B., Where Are You?

"**N**ow, where could she be?" said Calliope. She stood on the sidewalk in front of Mrs. B.'s house. The Dustbuster was cradled in her arms. Every so often she revved it.

It was a cloudless spring day, and Calliope stood still, listening for clues. A breeze rustled the trees and the high-pitched droning of peepers rose for a minute and then fell. Overhead, a plane roared. There was the faint sound of a lawn mower in the distance.

Calliope had never realized how noisy the world was. She'd always figured herself to be the main source of commotion on the street. Now she felt like a little wave among many big ones. Oh well, she was still young. There was plenty of time to learn how to be a big wave. Right now, though, she had to find Mrs. B.

Where the heck was she? Somewhere unexpected, for sure. Calliope let her imagination guide her.

She looked under the bushes in front of Mrs. B.'s house. She looked under the car parked on the street. She looked up the big elm tree in front of her house. She even checked a giant cardboard box, which sat upright in a puddle on the curb. Calliope kicked the box and then put her ear against it. All she heard was the droning of some peepers trapped inside.

Actually, Calliope heard something else. But it was not from inside the box. The new sound she heard was the faint sloshing of water. She immediately thought of the tin pail Mom kept in her garden behind the house.

Calliope rarely ventured into the backyard. But every Sunday—rain or shine—Mom headed stony-faced into her jungle. She'd emerge at the end of the day, smudged green and brown. There'd be dirt in her teeth and insects caught in her hair. Yet Mom would be smiling, smiling so hard it made you want to cry.

Calliope approached her backyard. She heard that faint sloshing again and saw a gray hair on the tip of a branch. Oh, Mrs. B. had really done it this time. She'd gone into Mom's jungle. There was no way she'd make it out alone. Calliope would have to go in there and get her. And Calliope didn't even have one of those funny helmets the white guys wore in Tarzan movies.

Calliope studied the thicket, which looked like an impenetrable green wall. Then she noticed the faint outline of a hunched figure. It was as if there were a secret doorway into Mom's jungle.

Imagining herself an African explorer, Calliope stepped through that doorway. The Dustbuster was her machete. With it, Calliope hacked at the thicket as she followed a trail of crushed leaves and broken branches.

Soon Calliope came to a small clearing. There was a rusty faucet, a tin pail of water and Mrs. B. She was on her knees, her face in the pail. Big bubbles burbled up through the water.

Boy, Mrs. B. sure was thirsty.

Face in the Bucket

Calliope bounced over and tapped Mrs. B. on the shoulder. Mrs. B. looked up. Long wet strands of gray hair covered her face. The front of her dress was soaked.

"Is it gone?" Mrs. B. mumbled.

Calliope dropped to her knees in front of Mrs. B. She squinted up into each of Mrs. B.'s nostrils. "I think so," she said.

Mrs. B. didn't look relieved, though. She looked like Mortimer after his monthly bath: wet and miserable.

Calliope took Mrs. B. by the hand and led her out of the garden. Calliope felt as though she were dragging a sack of potatoes.

Still, she forged on. She pushed back the brambles

with the Dustbuster. The branches bent forward and swung back, whacking Mrs. B. in the shins. But the old woman didn't even whimper. Boy, she really is down, thought Calliope. How could such a little ant cause so much trouble? Calliope smiled knowingly. Sometimes a little wave can make a big splash, she thought.

The two entered Calliope's house. Calliope led Mrs. B. to the couch, where she sat. Mrs. B. looked like a ship that had sprung a leak. She listed to the right. A puddle formed at her feet.

"Wait right here," said Calliope.

Mrs. Blatherhorn didn't reply.

Moments later Calliope returned with Mortimer cradled in her arms. She placed him gently in Mrs. Blatherhorn's lap. Mortimer tried to run, but Calliope held him in place. "Now, be a good boy and look after Mrs. B. for a minute."

Mortimer bared his teeth but settled down.

Calliope stepped back for a better view. Mrs. Blatherhorn still leaned right. Her hands lay palms up on the couch. She stared at the floor. Mortimer twitched in her lap.

This was not what Calliope had had in mind. She stepped toward Mrs. B. and placed Mrs. B.'s hand on Mortimer's head. "Now, that's better," Calliope declared. Mortimer gave her a dirty look, but Calliope shook her finger at him. "Behave," she ordered. She left for the kitchen.

Calliope climbed up on the counter and took a mug out of the cabinet. She filled the mug with water and grabbed a package of hot chocolate mix out of the pantry. Hot chocolate on a hot spring day? Of course! What better way to revive Mrs. B.'s spirits?

Calliope ripped open the hot chocolate package and turned it over. About half the mix fell in the cup. The other half fell on the counter. Oh well. Calliope figured she'd got enough in the cup to make the water at least taste chocolaty. She put the cup in the microwave, and when it went *ding,* Calliope rushed the steaming cup to Mrs. B.

Mrs. B. seemed to be feeling better already. She was still staring at the floor. But one hand stroked Mortimer's head.

Calliope put the hot chocolate in Mrs. B.'s other hand, which still lay on the couch. Mrs. B.'s fingers instinctively wrapped around the cup's handle. She raised the cup to her lips, sipping gingerly.

Her birdlike sips had an amazing effect. It was like in that movie. You know, the one where the mad scientist gives his monster life with a jolt of lightning. Doctor What's-his-name. Only this time Calliope was the mad scientist and Mrs. B. her creation.

Mrs. B.'s body jerked once, then again. Hot chocolate sloshed onto her dress but she didn't seem to mind. Her eyes brightened. She looked up from the floor at Mortimer, smiling.

Then Mrs. B. looked at Calliope and frowned. "I'm hungry," she barked. But this time she sounded like an excited puppy, not a bulldog.

Cheerios and Orange Juice

Calliope motioned for Mrs. B. to follow her.

Scooping up Mortimer, Mrs. B. stood and followed Calliope into the dinette.

Calliope sat Mrs. B. down at the head of the small table, as if she were the guest of honor. "Wait here and I'll get everything," she told Mrs. B.

Mrs. B. put Mortimer in her lap. She stroked Mortimer while looking around the small room.

Soon Calliope returned, her arms full. She carried a large box of Cheerios, a carton of orange juice, two tablespoons and two bowls. She set it all down in front of Mrs. B., who looked confused.

"Let me make it for you," Calliope said. She poured the Cheerios into the bowl and then filled the bowl with orange juice. Mrs. B. wrinkled up her nose.

"Oh no," Calliope said. "It's very good." She

spooned a big helping into her mouth. "Yum," she said, rubbing her stomach. She handed the spoon to Mrs. B.

"What do you think?" Mrs. B. asked Mortimer. His ears drooped and he rumbled softly, which means purr in rabbit. "Okay, okay," Mrs. B. said, and she ladled a big spoonful into her mouth. She crunched loudly. Orange juice trickled out the corner of her mouth.

"Well?" asked Calliope.

"Magnificent," mumbled Mrs. B. as she spooned in another mouthful.

Calliope joined Mrs. B. They hunkered over their bowls, munching. The small room echoed with the clinking of spoons against porcelain bowls.

Mrs. B. finished first. She picked up her bowl, slurping down the remaining orange juice.

Calliope looked on approvingly.

Mrs. Blatherhorn blushed when she noticed Calliope smiling at her.

"I bet your mother wouldn't have let you eat Cheerios with orange juice," said Calliope.

"Most certainly not!"

"Well, neither will mine."

"Your point?"

Calliope shrugged. "Don't get me wrong," she said. "Mom is great and all. But there's a time and place for parents. Don't you agree?"

Stroking Mortimer and savoring one last soggy juice-soaked Cheerio, Mrs. Blatherhorn had to admit she agreed.

Calliope pushed her bowl away and stood up. "Let's play," she said, slapping the table with both hands.

"All right," replied Mrs. Blatherhorn. "What do little girls play nowadays?"

"I know," Calliope said excitedly. "Let's burn ants!"

"Burn ants?" said Mrs. Blatherhorn, slightly horrified.

"Sure," said Calliope. "Don't you want"—she paused for emphasis—"revenge?"

"Revenge?" said Mrs. Blatherhorn, rolling the word around in her mouth. "What a lovely idea. How, then, do you burn ants?"

"First you need a magnifying glass," explained Calliope, trying to sound like a scientist. "Then you find an ant. You focus the sun on a little white dot on his bottom." She illustrated how little with her thumb and index finger.

"Of course, the ant tries to run—but it's no use. You keep that white dot of fire on him. Soon his body is smoking. He curls up, and *puff!* He's toast."

"Marvelous!" exclaimed Mrs. Blatherhorn. "Can Mortimer join us?"

"Of course!"

Fangs or No Fangs

Calliope dashed from the table and up the stairs. Halfway up she stopped. Mrs. B. was not behind her. Puzzled, Calliope returned to the dinette.

Mrs. B. stood at the table, cradling Mortimer. "Aren't you forgetting something?" she said, pointing Mortimer at the bowls on the table.

"Oh yeah," Calliope said sheepishly. She carried her bowl and Mrs. B.'s to the sink.

"Well?" asked Mrs. Blatherhorn, who had followed Calliope to the sink.

"Well what?" replied Calliope.

"Aren't you going to rinse them out and put them in the dishwasher?"

"Geez Louise," said Calliope. She grabbed a sponge and swished out the bowls. "I guess once a mother, always a mother," she muttered.

Calliope stopped and turned toward Mrs. Blatherhorn. "You did have children, right?"

"Oh yes. Three of them."

"Really?" said Calliope, eyes wide.

"One of them was once a little girl just like you."

"Why haven't I ever seen them?"

"They're all grown now."

"Don't they visit?"

"Rarely."

"Why not?"

"I guess I raised them too well," sighed Mrs. Blatherhorn. "They don't need me for anything. Nobody needs me."

Mrs. Blatherhorn sank to the floor. She sat, legs crossed, and hugged Mortimer.

"Oh, that's not true!" said Calliope, and sat down facing Mrs. Blatherhorn.

Mrs. Blatherhorn harrumphed.

"I need you," said Calliope.

"Oh yeah? For what?"

"Well, for starters, to get my fangs back."

"Your what?"

"My fangs," repeated Calliope, baring her teeth like Dracula.

Mortimer bared his teeth too.

"I see," said Mrs. Blatherhorn. "And who has these fangs?"

"Mrs. Perkins, my teacher," Calliope said. "She took them from me in class."

"And what were they doing in class?"

"I accidentally put them in my mouth during math."

"Accidentally?"

"Yes," explained Calliope. "My hand was bored, so it went off the desk and into my backpack. It took the fangs and put them in my mouth."

"Did you explain this to Mrs. What's-her-name?"

"It's Mrs. Perkins, and no way," Calliope said, sounding a bit sore. "She wouldn't understand."

"So how can I help?"

Calliope grinned. "Lend me your cane."

"My cane?"

"Just for an afternoon. I promise I won't hurt it."

"But why?"

"To float my fangs out of Mrs. Perkins' desk."

"I hate to disappoint, but that cane is nothing but a knobby old piece of wood," said Mrs. Blatherhorn. "It couldn't raise the hair on the back of your teacher's neck."

Calliope sighed. She sounded like a balloon losing air. "You're not really a witch, are you?"

"I'm afraid not," said Mrs. Blatherhorn. She studied Calliope, who sagged.

"But I do act like one sometimes, don't I?" said

Mrs. Blatherhorn. She bared her teeth for Calliope and snarled.

Calliope couldn't help laughing.

"Look," said Mrs. Blatherhorn. "So what if I'm not a real witch? We can still pretend, can't we?" Mrs. Blatherhorn turned to Mortimer and repeated, "Can't we?"

"Oh yes!" said Calliope.

"And you can be my apprentice!"

Mortimer kicked Mrs. Blatherhorn in the stomach.

"Oh yes—and you too, Mortimer."

Calliope suddenly frowned.

"What's wrong?" asked Mrs. Blatherhorn. "You don't want Mortimer to be an apprentice too?"

"Oh no. It's not that," said Calliope.

"Then what?"

"We can't really get my fangs back, can we?"

"Why, sure we can!"

"But how?"

"I'm a witch, remember? Now, listen closely. Here are your first magic words."

Calliope leaned forward and Mrs. B. whispered in her ear.

"That's it?" said Calliope.

Mrs. B. nodded.

"Say 'I'm sorry'?" Calliope said the words as if she were sucking a sourball.

"Yes, you'd be surprised at how well it works. Let me demonstrate. I'm sorry."

"For what?"

"For calling the police, for harassing poor little Mortimer and trying to run your family off the street."

Calliope looked surprised.

"Oh, don't play dumb," said Mrs. Blatherhorn. "I saw you looking at my hit list."

Calliope confessed. "I didn't need that stupid list. I knew it all along."

"You knew?"

"Yep."

"How?"

"I don't know. I just did."

Mrs. B. nodded. "Maybe it's *you* who's a witch."

Yeah, thought Calliope. Maybe I am.

"Come here," said Mrs. B. "Give me a hug."

Calliope squeezed Mrs. B. so hard that Mrs. B. leaked water like a sponge. It dripped on Mortimer, who squirmed out between Calliope and Mrs. B.

"He doesn't like mushy stuff," said Calliope as she and Mrs. B. watched Mortimer hop back to his cage.

Calliope released Mrs. B. and stood up. Pointing toward the ceiling, she said, "It's time for revenge!"

Smoking
Ant Butts

Calliope led Mrs. B. upstairs to her room. At the doorway, Mrs. B. stopped. She looked at all the shoeboxes.

"Don't be afraid," said Calliope. She pulled Mrs. B. by the hand to her bed. They stood over a box filled with magnifying glasses.

Calliope picked up a magnifying glass lying on top. Its smudged lens was as big as a pancake. Calliope held the lens up to her eye. The lens made her eye look like something out of *Science Fiction Theater*.

"No good," Calliope pronounced, and tossed the lens back in the box. She picked up a smaller one with a shiny white handle.

Mrs. Blatherhorn peered over Calliope's shoulder. "How do you tell one from the other?" she asked. "They all look the same to me."

"Easy," said Calliope. "Allow me to demonstrate."

She raised her window shade, letting the sun stream into her room. Standing next to the window, she held the magnifying glass so that it made a white dot on her hand. She moved the lens up and down until the dot was a tight little circle.

"See how small but sharp that dot is?" said Calliope.

Mrs. Blatherhorn nodded.

"The smaller the dot, the hotter— *Youch!*" hollered Calliope. She tossed the lens, shaking her hand. "Now, that's a good one."

She offered to let Mrs. Blatherhorn try out a magnifying glass.

"No thanks, dear," Mrs. Blatherhorn replied. "I'll take your word for it."

Calliope rooted around in the lens box. "Aha!" She pulled out a large one with a skull and crossbones on its handle. "This is one of my personal favorites," she said, handing it to Mrs. Blatherhorn.

"I'm honored," said Mrs. Blatherhorn.

Calliope took a lens with a glittering green handle.

Magnifying glasses in hand, the two went outside. They stood on the walkway in front of Calliope's house.

"Now, where do we find these ants?" said Mrs. Blatherhorn.

Calliope pointed to the ground and squatted. She waddled along the walkway, studying every brick. Soon she found a big black ant with a fat rear end. A lovely target.

Calliope held her magnifying glass over the ant, zeroing in on its rump. The ant began racing in circles, but Calliope's aim held true. Within seconds there was a whiff of smoke and the big ant was a cinder.

"Ah, smell that?" said Calliope.

Mrs. Blatherhorn sniffed. Her nose tingled with the faint smell of burned match heads.

"There's nothing like the smell of charred ant butt," said Calliope.

"It's my turn," said Mrs. Blatherhorn, squatting next to Calliope. Her knees cracked loudly.

"Are you all right?" asked Calliope.

"That's nothing," said Mrs. Blatherhorn. "You should hear me get out of bed in the morning. I sound like a creaky old wooden ship in a high wind. Now, where's an ant?"

Mrs. Blatherhorn's head moved back and forth as she searched the ground at her feet.

"There's one!" said Calliope, pointing at a big fat black ant. It had stopped at Mrs. Blatherhorn's feet. Calliope swore she saw that ant look up, antennae twitching nervously.

Mrs. Blatherhorn raised her lens and the ant took

off. This one is no dummy, thought Calliope. It raced in a curlicue pattern that Mrs. Blatherhorn couldn't follow. "Darn," she said.

"Let me help," said Calliope, grabbing Mrs. Blatherhorn's wrist. She gently guided her hand. Mrs. Blatherhorn's lens again found the ant, but the battle had just begun.

"He's a clever one," said Calliope, nodding in appreciation. Indeed, that ant seemed to know every trick in the ant book. He turned this way and that, doubled back on himself, ran up weeds and dived into cracks between the bricks.

But in the end he was no match for Calliope. She held Mrs. Blatherhorn's lens in relentless pursuit. Soon he was smoking too. And *puff!* He was gone.

"Gotcha!" shouted Mrs. Blatherhorn. She slapped her thigh and did a funny little dance that Calliope imagined ducks might do when humans weren't looking.

"Can I ask you something?" said Calliope.

"Sure, dear. Anything."

"When that ant was up your nose, what did it feel like?"

Mrs. Blatherhorn grabbed her nose for a moment and got a funny look. "Do you really want to know?"

Calliope nodded enthusiastically.

"Well, let's see," said Mrs. Blatherhorn. "It was as if there were a little man up my nose."

"Really?"

"Oh yes," said Mrs. Blatherhorn, warming to her description. "And he was a very rude little man, I might add. He stomped. He bit. He yanked on my nose hairs."

Calliope wrinkled up her nose. "Sounds awful. Did it hurt?"

"Actually, no."

"I bet you were scared anyway," said Calliope.

"More than I've ever been," Mrs. Blatherhorn said solemnly.

"Were you afraid? Afraid it would crawl into your brain?"

"Oh no, it wasn't that," said Mrs. Blatherhorn.

Calliope looked puzzled.

"I was scared I was going to laugh," explained Mrs. Blatherhorn. No sooner had she spoken these words than she started to giggle.

"Oh my," she said, clapping a hand over her mouth. It didn't help, though. Her giggling grew louder and more uncontrollable, like a bad case of the hiccups.

To Calliope, Mrs. B.'s giggling sounded like a glass of cola. All fizzy. It made Calliope feel warm and light-headed. Soon she was giggling too. Her giggles became laughter.

Calliope and Mrs. B. laughed and they laughed. Mrs. Blatherhorn toppled over onto the lawn. She rolled around, kicking and pounding her fists. Dirt and brown grass flew everywhere. Mrs. B. had turned into a dust devil.

And Mrs. B. says she's no witch, thought Calliope. Hah! And hah! again. Maybe Mrs. B. was no witch, but she was wicked, all right. Wickedly funny. She was the funniest thing Calliope had ever seen.

Calliope let herself fall backward into the grass. The scratchy blades tickled her neck and she laughed more loudly.

Calliope's eyes got all watery. She blinked, and blinked again. But her eyes wouldn't clear. It was as if she were on the bottom of a swimming pool looking up.

Mrs. B. and Calliope rolled and laughed until they could laugh no more. Exhausted, they lay face up, side by side. They held hands and looked up at the big puffy clouds moving slowly across the blue sky.

"Mrs. B.?"

"Yes?"

"Would you come to my class?"

"Aren't I a bit old, dear?"

"Yes . . . I mean no."

Mrs. Blatherhorn raised herself up on an elbow and looked down into Calliope's face.

"I made this bet with my teacher," said Calliope.

"A bet? About me?"

"Well," Calliope paused, searching for the right

words. Ah, heck. Why not say it right out? "I bet you were a witch."

"I see," said Mrs. B. thoughtfully. "So it's time to put up or shut up."

"Exactly."

Mrs. B., the Witch

"You may begin," said Mrs. Perkins. She sat on her high stool. In front of her were Calliope and Mrs. B., who wore high heels and a long black dress.

They stood side by side, facing the class. Mrs. B. leaned on her cane. But she had turned it backward so that no one could see the snarling head—at least not yet.

In front of them was a small table draped in black cloth. On top of the table was a tall black hat with a red band.

Calliope looked out at the class. She felt some twenty-odd pairs of eyes boring into her. Oh, boy. Maybe this hadn't been such a good idea. She glanced at Mrs. B., who smiled back weakly.

Mrs. Perkins loudly cleared her throat.

Uh-oh, thought Calliope. It's showtime. Well, here

goes. "This," said Calliope, pointing at Mrs. B., "is my good friend, Mrs. B."

Mrs. B. smiled ever so slightly.

"Mrs. B. may look like a grandma, talk like a grandma— Say something," said Calliope to Mrs. B., jabbing her in the ribs.

"Ouch," said Mrs. B.

The class giggled.

"Children," said Mrs. Perkins. She clapped her hands three times.

The class quieted.

"Like I was saying," continued Calliope. "Mrs. B. may look like a grandma, but she's not."

"She's not?" blurted Noreen, who sat in the first row.

Calliope glared at Noreen. "No, she's not."

"Then what is she?"

Calliope smiled wickedly. "She's a witch. The Witch of Hummingbird Lane."

Mrs. B. raised an eyebrow and leaned over to whisper in Calliope's ear. "I don't live on Hummingbird Lane."

"I know," Calliope whispered back. "But it sounds nice, don't you think?"

Calliope glanced back at Mrs. Perkins. The teacher slowly shook her head but said nothing.

Calliope turned again toward the class and heard

snickering. In the back, someone called out, "Yeah, right."

The class broke up in laughter.

Calliope's face reddened and she scanned the rows of little faces. Aha! So it was Thomas. Her arm shot out, pointing at him. "Give him the evil eye!" she shouted.

Mrs. B. nodded. She narrowed her eyes until they were slits. The slits followed Calliope's pointing finger to the boy. Mrs. B. glared at him and gave a low growl.

Thomas's face turned white, and he sank low into his seat.

"Okay," said Calliope, slapping her hands together. "Now, who wants to see my witch pull a magic rabbit out of this hat?"

Some twenty-odd hands shot up.

"All right then," said Calliope. She stepped out in front of the table. Cupping both hands in front of her mouth, she tooted out an introductory song. Then she swept a hand grandly toward Mrs. B. "Ladies and gentlemen, I give you the great Witch of Hummingbird Lane."

Mrs. B. nodded slightly and then raised her cane, pointing its snarling face toward the class. She moved the head slowly from left to right and back again. All eyes followed that head.

Holding the cane lengthwise in both hands, Mrs. B. raised it over her head. Her eyes closed. In a gravelly voice, Mrs. B. chanted, "Hoggily, woggily, pudding pie. Make me a rabbit by and by."

"Oh, brother," muttered Mrs. Perkins.

Calliope spun around, a finger against her lips. "Shhh!"

Mrs. Perkins glared back but said nothing.

Mrs. B. ignored Calliope and Mrs. Perkins. With eyes closed, she lowered one hand into the hat. Her other hand held the cane high.

The children leaned forward in their seats.

Calliope folded her arms and smiled a smile that seemed to say *I told you so.*

Her smile didn't last long.

You see, Mrs. B. was new at this witch stuff. And her magic tricks, well, they needed a little work.

By now Mrs. B. had her whole arm in the hat. She turned toward Calliope, frowning.

"Allow me," said Calliope. She leaned across the table and looked into the hat. "Mortimer," she whispered sternly.

The class began to giggle.

Calliope looked at her classmates and stuck out her tongue.

The giggling grew louder.

Mrs. B. withdrew her arm, and Calliope put her

face into the hat. "Mortimer. You come out here this minute."

There was no response from the hat.

"All right, you asked for it," said Calliope. She picked up the hat and turned it upside down. Nothing came out. She banged the bottom of the hat and then shook it.

Still nothing came out. But this time Calliope heard something. Something that reminded her of her radiator. Yes, it was a low hiss, rising slowly in pitch. And it was coming from somewhere in the classroom.

"Make it stop," said Mrs. Perkins. She covered her ears with both hands.

Geez, Mrs. Perkins sure is sensitive to high noises, thought Calliope. What does she do in the winter, when the radiators kick in? Freeze?

No time to think about that now, though. Calliope dropped to her knees in front of the table. She threw back the black cloth. Underneath was Mortimer's cage. It was empty.

"Oh, great," said Calliope. She dropped to her hands and knees and crawled around the front of the classroom. "Mortimer, oh, Mortimer," she called.

Children stood, trying to see Calliope. Some of them climbed on top of their desks.

Mrs. Perkins didn't say a thing—except "Make it stop, make it stop."

All right, already. Calliope was trying as hard as she could. She looked at Mrs. B., who now stood away from the table. One hand rested on the cane. The other tried to cover a big smile.

"Do you mind?" said Calliope. "I could use some help down here."

"Sorry," said Mrs. B. "Of course." She slowly lowered herself to all fours and began crawling behind Calliope. The cane clunked on the floor as Mrs. B. crawled.

"Mortimer, oh, Mortimer," the two of them called. They headed toward Mrs. Perkins' desk. The hissing grew louder.

Mrs. B. spurted ahead of Calliope and crawled under the big wooden desk. "Aha!" she called out. "There's the little rascal."

Calliope crawled in after Mrs. B. She saw Mortimer in a far, dark corner. He wore a little black cape. Some paper cutout fangs dangled by tape from his lower jaw.

Mortimer's head was cocked back. His teeth were bared. Reverberating under the desk, the hissing sound was almost unbearable.

Calliope grabbed Mortimer, pulling him to her chest. She crawled out from under the desk and stood up. She held her rabbit out to the class.

The children clapped loudly.

Calliope bowed. Mrs. B. stood, and Calliope motioned for her to bow too.

Then Calliope remembered Mrs. Perkins. She put her hand over Mortimer's mouth and he stopped hissing.

Mrs. Perkins put her hands down and sighed. She looked around wide-eyed, noticing the standing children for the first time.

"Well?" said Calliope.

"Well, what?" answered Mrs. Perkins.

"Do I win the bet or what?"

Mrs. Perkins sat up and straightened her blouse. "She couldn't even pull the rabbit out of the hat," she huffed.

Mrs. B. narrowed her eyes again. She raised her cane, pointing the menacing head at Mrs. Perkins. "Grrr," Mrs. B. growled.

Mrs. Perkins sniffed and looked away.

"Down, girl," said Calliope, raising a hand to lower Mrs. B.'s cane. "Let me handle this."

Calliope removed her hand from Mortimer's mouth. He threw back his head and made like a boiling teakettle again.

"All right, all right," pleaded Mrs. Perkins.

Calliope covered Mortimer's mouth and he stopped.

Mrs. Perkins stood and walked over to her desk.

Mrs. B. and Calliope stepped aside. They watched Mrs. Perkins open a bottom drawer, taking out a wad of dusty crumpled tissues. She removed the tissues and held up a pair of pink fangs.

Calliope jumped up and down.

Mrs. Perkins gave Calliope a dirty look.

"Well?" said Mrs. B.

Mrs. Perkins raised the fangs. She wrinkled up her nose, closed her eyes and opened her mouth. In went the fangs. Mrs. Perkins closed her mouth and spun around to face the class. The look in her eye silenced the children. Mrs. Perkins raised her hands like claws. Her mouth opened and she hissed and snapped viciously. Then she closed her mouth. Two sharp pink teeth hung out over her bottom lip.

The class exploded in applause. Mrs. B. clapped along with the children and exclaimed, "Bravissimo!"

Calliope
Comes Clean

"**D**o I have to?" whispered Calliope. She stood in the doorway of Mom's bedroom. Her mother sat, head down, paying bills at a desk.

"Go on," said Mrs. Blatherhorn. She stood behind Calliope and gave her a little push into the bedroom.

"All right, all right. I'm going."

Mom looked up at the sound of Calliope's voice. She started to smile but stopped midway at the sight of Mrs. Blatherhorn. "Now what?"

Calliope inched into the room, one arm extended. In her hand was a crumpled piece of paper. "Here."

Mom took the paper and unfolded it. Her eyes got big as she saw what was written on the paper.

" 'I.O.U. two thousand, six hundred ninety-three dollars'?" she read aloud.

"Uh . . . it's a refund."

"For what?"

"All the ASPs you paid for—but I didn't go to."

"Calliope," Mom said in a rising voice.

"I'll pay you back, honest."

"I don't care about the money."

"I know," said Calliope, hanging her head. Her eyes began to tear.

"If you weren't in school, where were you?"

"Home."

"Alone?"

"Yes."

Mom threw up her hands.

Calliope looked up, teary-eyed. "I'm sorry, Mom."

"This must never, never happen again."

"It won't. I promise."

Mom looked skeptical.

"I'm never staying after school again."

"Calliope—"

"I don't have to, Mom," Calliope interrupted. "Mrs. B. will stay with me."

"Oh, she will?" Mom looked up at Mrs. Blatherhorn.

"It's quite all right," said Mrs. Blatherhorn.

"I don't know," said Mom. "She's quite a handful, as you can see."

"Oh yes, I know," agreed Mrs. Blatherhorn. "But trust me. I can handle her." She raised a hand, claw-like, and growled at Calliope.

Calliope fell to her knees. "Please, no more, no more." Then she and Mrs. B. cackled.

"See?" said Mrs. Blatherhorn, looking at Mom. "Everything's under control."

Mom stared at the two of them.

Calliope walked on her knees over to Mom. She put a wet cheek against the hand resting in Mom's lap. "Please, oh please, oh please."

Mom drummed her fingers under Calliope's cheek and stared at Mrs. Blatherhorn.

Mrs. B. barked once and then smiled sweetly.

"You must be a witch," said Mom, looking at the old woman and then down at her groveling daughter. "How else can I explain this?"

Mom pulled the hand in her lap free and shook a finger at Calliope. "You're to come straight home after school, understand?"

"Yes," Calliope said softly.

"And your homework is to be done when I get home from work."

"Absolutely," said Mrs. Blatherhorn.

Mom slumped in her chair and then threw out both arms. "Give me a hug."

Calliope stood up and threw herself into Mom's arms. This time her tears were real.